Memoirs of Leticia Valle

Rosa Chacel

Memoirs of

Leticia Valle

(Memorias de Leticia Valle)

Translated and with an Afterword by Carol Maier

University of Nebraska Press : Lincoln and London

Library of Congress
Cataloging in Publication Data
Chacel, Rosa, 1898–
[Memorias de Leticia Valle.
English] Memoirs of
Leticia Valle / Rosa Chacel :
translated and with
an afterword by Carol Maier.
p. cm.
ISBN 0-8032-1456-1 (cl)
ISBN 0-8032-6360-0 (pa)
1. Title.
PQ7797.C412M413 1994
863-DC20 93-25205 CIP

Contents

Memoirs of Leticia Valle

On March 10 I will be twelve years old. I don't know why, but that's all I've been able to think about for several days. What does it matter to me if I'm twelve or fifty? I guess I think about it because, if I didn't, what would I think about?

I do not think about all those things from before; I see them inside me; every one of my minutes is one of those minutes, but thinking, when I'm thinking, when I start to think, I have only one thought: on March 10 I will be twelve years old. The trouble is, when I'm thinking I ask myself: what's going to happen? Nothing is going to happen. The days will just keep going by until it's March 10, and I do know what will happen on that day. Then there will be more days again with nothing different.

When I try to tell myself something about all that happened, I can only think of the phrase my father used: 'It's inconceivable, it's inconceivable.' I can almost see him in his corner, deep in his armchair, holding his forehead with one hand, repeating that phrase while, from my chair, I tell him without telling him: 'That's what I was always trying to tell you. I did not know how to say that everything about me was inconceivable, but I tried to make you understand, while you kept saying there was nothing special about it. So now if you say what happened seems inconceivable it's because you still believe there was nothing special about it before.'

But what good is all this discussion? We're miles apart from each other, just like we always were, except that now distance is an advantage for me: it isolates me, it belongs to me, and I don't have the same craving for explanations. Before, when I talked about my things, it was as if I were asking people to protect me from them. Now, the worst of those things don't scare me. I can dare to repeat them here, I will even write them down so they will never be erased in my memory. And it's not to make myself feel better: I need to look at myself mirrored in those things and see myself surrounded by everything I worshiped, everything they have separated me from, as if those things had hurt me. Here, no one can take those things from me, and they can't get away either; here, those things will be however I want, and they can't do anything to me. Neither can these other things, the ones really around me; I see them, but I refuse to believe them.

Even so, what's happening to me is the same as what's happening to the branch of ivy that has grown up to the frame of my window. When I look at it out of the corner of my eye and see it peering in at the glass, the branch looks like a lizard that would run away if I got too close. It's not what it seems, though; it can't run away or tremble, even if I rap on the glass with my knuckles. Still, I like to believe we're companions. The ivy's life is so slow; even slower than the clock hands I've often watched for hours in hopes of seeing them advance. Here that branch is what will measure my time. As I watch, it keeps advancing, just the same as when I forget it or when I'm sleeping; right now it's about level with the largest knot in the wood, and I know that by March 10 it will have grown a few inches, or perhaps more.

Whatever I grow between then and now will be even less noticeable. Adriana tells me that soon, since it's almost the end of October, those slopes will be covered with snow and we'll go skiing, that any minute her music teacher will be here and we'll have music class in her mother's sitting room, that I have to hurry up and learn German so I can study along with her. I will not learn German or go skiing or study anything. I will not follow the path they've set out for me; I will not walk at that pace; I'll go in another direction, up or down, escaping however I can, and they won't even realize it. They'll see me every day in the same place with my feet still, but I won't be here: I'll be going backwards; it's the only thing I can do. How could they ever understand this? I won't do anything conspicuous, they won't even see me lift a finger; I'll turn all my efforts inside, I'll run backwards until I'm breathless, until I get to the end, until I get lost. Then I'll return here and go back again.

No, I'll never get here. It seems easier to get there, to reach the beginning. As for all the rest, whatever's on the right or the left, I can take it or leave it, and I'll only take what I really want. Not what I want as a whim but what I want with all my heart, what I want with the wanting that comes from the beginning; from God that must be, since God is the beginning and the end of everything. I still don't know enough to think about this on my own, and yet a long time ago, when I still knew absolutely nothing, I was already thinking it. I always felt it this way. When I pray, above all when I pray in the dark, when I lie in bed facing the wall and test the darkness with my eyes, moving them in all directions and not seeing anything, until I'm convinced that I don't see anything, I still can't think of anything. Sometimes I'm not even sure if my eyes are open or closed and I touch myself slowly, very slowly, with the tip of a finger, as if to discover an eye that was not mine; and when I touch the corner of my eye between my eyelashes, and convince myself that it's open, then I'm sure I don't see anything and I experience a moment of terrible anxiety, but finally I begin the Lord's Prayer.

I have such a tremendous need to think for myself that when

3

I can't, when I have to content myself with an idea that does not originate in me, I accept it with such indifference I feel like a creature with no feelings. This really tortures me when I try to formulate some idea of what my mother must have been like. When I was little, I used to hear people talk about her and I would say to myself: No, that's not what she was like, I remember something quite different; but what is it I remembered? Nothing, of course, nothing you can talk about, not even obscurely. The truth is I could never remember what my mother was like, but I remember being in bed with her, it must have been summer, and I would wake up and I could feel the skin of my face all stuck to her arm and the palm of my hand stuck to her breast. No matter how many years go by, this memory will never be erased, and I can sink into it so intensely, in particular, in a way so exactly like things happened when the memory was reality, that I do not seem to be looking at it from further and further away. On the contrary, it seems that some day I will overtake it. Now I study it, thinking it over again and again; before, I would look at it, I would spend hours observing it over and over.

What I seemed to feel was exactly no feeling somewhere, like having a part of me lost or blind. It was as if I were sticking to something that, although it was the same as me, was immense, endless, something so large I knew I would never be able to know all of it, and then, although that sensation was delightful, I would feel a tremendous desire to provoke a shift of position, to emerge on my own, and I would grab hold of myself, pull on myself from I don't know where, and finally come unstuck. I remember the very faint sound my skin made as it separated from hers, like the tearing of very fine tissue paper. I remember how I hovered in the air a bit as I sat up, and I must have looked at her then and she probably looked at me. Yes, I know she would have looked at me, smiled at me, said something to me; I no longer remember any of this.

4

It's strange: if I remember what I felt, why don't I remember what I saw? I believe it must be because I've continued to see more and more things since then; on the other hand, I never again felt anything similar to that.

Everyone, more or less everybody in the whole world, must have felt something comparable, but if they have all felt it why don't they talk about it? Of course I haven't talked about it either, but when other people talk I look between their words for a hint that might suggest some familiarity with it, and I never find one. They obviously have a different point of departure; they talk about other things. They talk about the way mothers love, about things mothers do and stop doing, and I always say deep inside me: that was love.

Yes, since then, other people have done things for me, everyone has loved me, sacrificed for me, as they say, but that other thing has nothing to do with these sacrifices. These I neither understand nor want to understand, although they must be clear. That was like water, or like sky. It was so wonderful there! And a person wanted to leave in order to feel even better exactly how it was.

Aside from that, I don't remember anything good about those years. Only the anguish of having to learn some things in order to understand others, because most of the time people talk in a way that at first makes it hard to know what's expected of you. They're so apt to give a stupid explanation for the most mysterious things, so likely to cover those things up, disguise them with a mystery that is odious.

I spent four or five years hearing, but not understanding, how my father had gone to Africa to get himself killed by the Moors. I would compare how serious that sounded to me with how offhandedly people said it, and I could never manage to reconcile that difference. Then I would think: either it's not so serious or it's something acceptable, and my inability to decide never stopped bothering me. It was not impossible for me to understand that my father might want to die, but why would he want to get himself killed by the Moors? Besides, why did they say it with that mystery, that tone? When I asked, they would answer by shrugging their shoulders or shaking their heads, and I felt embarrassed, although I don't know if it was because of my father or because of myself, because of my own inability to understand, because I couldn't grasp the heart of whatever it was they didn't want to tell me. The papers would come and I used to watch everyone's faces as they read the news and sighed with relief because they didn't find what we all feared, but then they would shake their heads as if to say: nothing, he's still accomplished nothing . . .

I lived with the discomfort of not understanding that, and many times I forgot about it, but suddenly it would come back into my head and I felt so close, it seemed so certain I was going to understand at any minute, that I would blush. Not from embarrassment, though, from emotion, as if something frightened me, I don't know what. My heart would beat furiously, a warmth would spread across my forehead, clouding my eyes, and I would feel as if I had struck the truth, even though I could not manage to formulate anything new or clear. What I found most nauseating was the covering other people put over that truth and the explanations, always those explanations about my father and mother. Always those pronouncements: 'If you really love another person you always do such and such; love is not like that, it's like this.' And the only thing I could do was say inside, with all my desperation and disgust: 'You idiots, that was love!'

Fortunately, I spent most of the time with my Aunt Aurelia, who was the least talkative. You could really say we lived alone, since the housekeeper and servants kept to themselves toward the middle of the house, and almost no one came to visit us.

There were periods when my professor came very punctually every morning, then there would be periods of several days when she did not come at all. Both she and the doctor said I knew too much and it was better for me to take walks than study. My poor aunt took me out every day and we always stopped at my grandmother's house before or after our walk. The really important conversations occurred at that house, around the table, which was heated underneath with a foot-warmer. My aunts amused themselves making Irish lace and doing Tenerife openwork; they had the room overflowing with their frames and little baskets. I felt as if I would suffocate in there, and one of my tricks for getting to leave sooner was asking my grandmother if there were any errands for us. She took this as a sign that I was particularly anxious to please her and she saved us the most difficult errands. We always had to buy special things for her in the strangest places or spend hours explaining something that needed to be made to order. My aunt was the one who placed the orders, but I was the one who had to take them from my grandmother because everyone trusted my prodigious memory.

I was especially happy when we had to go to the pharmacy; since my grandmother was used to certain old prescriptions and she had so many demands and requirements, the military pharmacy was the only place they would prepare her medications. When my aunt and I went there, we never knew how long it might be before we could get the druggist by himself and tell him that in the last refill there had been too much or too little of one thing or another. While we waited, I walked through the arcade where the pharmacy was located.

Time spent waiting is wonderful; it seems as though you are not in yourself, that you are doing something for someone else, and yet you are so free.

That arcade was at the entrance to Obispo Street, but it

turned in the middle so the exit was on Sierpe Street, and at the bend there was a rotunda that had a skylight with glass panes and four statues representing the seasons, with Mercury in the middle. The light falling over that small enclosed plaza was wonderful! At any hour, any time of year, the light there made you understand. I don't know why, but I understood history from there. From there, the history I did not like to study in books seemed to be something divine. Walking round and round between those statues, under that light, my thoughts adapted themselves to the day. If it was during the summer, a little before twelve, the sun was terrible, irritating, and tragic. Then I would think about the gladiators who died in the Roman circus. Most of all I saw the ones who died as they stepped on the net; I saw their bodies dragged through the sand, and also something I read, although I can't remember where: two of them who died at the same time, piercing each other with their swords. Beneath that sun, beneath that heartbreaking light, this was the scene I always saw: two naked men killing each other at the same time. If I was there during siesta, I would think about things from America, about hummingbirds and hammocks. I would see a woman dressed in white, sleeping in the shade of a canebrake, with a black butterfly resting on the middle of her chest. If it was early in the morning, I thought about Greece, especially when the arcade had just been hosed down and there were small pools with a fresh feeling like music; then I thought mostly about Narcissus. Other times, when it was raining, I would think about the Beer King. I don't know why he was called that, nor where I had gotten that character, but I loved him. When the light was gray and all you could hear was the rain on the glass in the skylight, I would see him seated on a chair with a very high back, with grape leaves carved in the wood. He was in an immense room with Gothic windows and in one corner there was a keg with a paunch so perfect it looked alive. But him! . . . I knew every detail of what he was like. He was dressed in velvet, it was not always the same color, but it was always trimmed with sable. I could not imagine him without that. Two belts of skins hung from his shoulders, and between them you could see his chest wonderfully rose-colored and very broad; he wore a lace shirt with a square frill under his red beard. His mouth glistened through the hairs of his beard when he smiled, especially when he ate the small fried fish he picked up with his fingertips by the heads and the tails. This is the pose I imagined him in most often: seated before a huge table and eating one of those little fish. He would bite it on the spine, taking the flesh from it with his teeth, and I always saw the first bite, which was in the middle, at a point something like the waist of the fish. While he ate, he would gaze into space with blue eyes that were almost smiling. I don't know who he might have been smiling at, because I always saw him alone in that great room. Other times he sat with his knees apart and his feet together on a cushion, beside the keg, watching a golden stream fall from the spigot into a beer mug, his eyes half closed, like a dozing cat.

I don't know if all these things I imagined in the arcade can be called History. The thing is, I felt I learned a lot there. I had these daydreams everywhere, but when I was not there they were very different. Some of the daydreams kept me company when we went visiting, others I had in bed before falling asleep, others in church. The ones I had on visits were generally about tiny little people I would see suddenly on a piece of furniture, in a corner where at times I would discover just the right setting for them. My aunt often took me to the house of some friends, two unmarried sisters who were very old; the younger one played the piano and practiced every afternoon for several hours. When we arrived at her house, she would keep practicing, and I would stay with her, seated on the carpet, in a corner next to the console table, while my aunt talked with the other one in the sitting room. One day I asked her what she was playing and she told me she was reviewing the fugues. She played very well; her music was so light, so clean. While she practiced I thought about other things, but sometimes one section would stand out and catch my attention, leaving me surprised or dazzled, like when you're looking absentmindedly at the sky and suddenly there's a star shooting by.

The things I thought in that room were all like those fugues, they were always light, transparent things. I would see a white horse running on the seat of an armchair covered with green velvet. Its skin was like mother-of-pearl, it had black eyes, and it would throw back its mane, tossing its head the way a little girl does. Once I saw it stop and remove the lock of hair from its forehead with its hand. Yes, with its hand, that's what I saw. I also saw some shiny patches in the black wood under the claws of the console table, some dark corners, some changes of light and shadow that were like a black world illuminated by a black sun. In that place there were always two very small beings who were white and transparent like fairies; they hugged each other and they loved each other a lot.

All of these things I saw without taking part in them, although I felt all kinds of feelings, as well as the mood where the things took place. On the other hand, in the fantasies I had in church I always saw myself transformed, doing impossible things, but entirely myself.

I had favorite images and corners in all the churches of Valladolid, but in San Sebastian there was that Christ in a glass case, asleep on His white pillow embroidered with gold. I could never pray to Him, I don't like prayers; only the Lord's Prayer, and you don't say it to Christ. I would kneel there and try to get close to Him, but that was all; it was an enormous effort that required my whole imagination. I left myself, I lived, breathed the air moving inside the glass panes that guarded Him, I watched the sparkle of His eyes between their half-closed lids, the corners of His mouth where something like a scent seemed to escape.

My usual place was in the middle of the stairway located at the head of the altar, but I could not always manage to get myself really inside the glass case. I always imagined being able to do it, always concentrated on the idea of walking around inside, on the idea that I had shrunk to fit in the small space beside His body, but sometimes it was not imagination: I entered there totally, with all my five senses. Then those dark purple shadows around His eyes, on His cheeks, on His temples, seemed to be moving. They were no longer a coloring or a complexion He had, they were like something that appeared, something that passed over Him. I felt Him suffer it, I buried my eyes in those shadows of His agony as if they were dark, deep water that had been agitated world without end, and my heart beat faster thinking about that eternal agitation, that torture moving those shadows like black wings. And then I would feel a need to rest, to sleep while I watched them move, to let my head fall on His chest while they went on fluttering.

That was not thinking, I think now, in order to push my memories to their limit; then it was something different, something totally different. What I saw at those times I did not call shadows, and I did not try to take a particular position: I felt I was there, I *was* there, I let go of myself, forgot myself there, until something happened within me that could only be compared to a flow of tears. Something wept within me, a thread of tears ran through a place like the hiding place of my soul, brief as a flash of lightning. I would never have confessed this to anyone: it was like a terrible secret, although at the same time one I was proud of. To confess it, however, would have been to reveal that I was not a child. Long before I was seven I carried the weight of this secret.

When I was eight they decided to send me to the school run by the Carmelites so I would have some contact with other little girls, and there my secret proved overwhelming. I began to see what girls were like.

When they talked about me, the members of my family always spoke with the same mystery as when they talked about my father, as if they knew what I had in my head and it was something so dreadful it could not even be mentioned by name. They sent me there as if to cure me of something: so I would learn to be a little girl, they said. But when I began to know little girls, they gave me a sense of horror, horror and disgust. They were the ones who were sick, and their sickness was childhood. Some of them seemed incapable of doing anything; nothing they tried to do turned out, as if they weren't completely awake. Others, on the other hand, had learned everything they needed to learn; it wasn't a question of lessons. The way they were always smashing bricks and dividing up the pieces! At recess I would see them playing with those pieces and fixing their little pretend meals and I would have liked to step on them. Nevertheless, I behaved myself. I never fought with anyone; I only watched until my eyes bulged, and no one ever knew why.

Even though I watched them so much I've forgotten them almost completely. Of all of them only one stands out for me, and I'll never forget her. That girl was the only one who had a secret, like me. But we could never have joined our secrets. She had nothing in common with me, my God, no. How was I later able to think she did? That idea was nothing other than a desire for punishment. It was the penitence I imposed on myself. Once I believed there was some resemblance between us, because people were able to come to the same conclusion about both of us, because our housekeeper, who is nothing more than an old woman full of bad habits and nasty feelings, wanted to wrap me in the same shroud that Sister, another old hag, used about her.

But how could that be? Where's the resemblance? I would ask everyone. I will never understand it. And yet it hurts me, it drives me crazy to remember their voices so full of experience, saying that, spitting that out.

I despised the girl: she seemed cross-eyed to me even though she was not. Everything about her squinted, her postures, her body, her feet. She sat on her kidneys, with her legs apart, and the points of her toes turned inward. At sewing time she would go into a corner and not take one stitch: she licked the wall. I don't know what she was up to over there, but one thing I did see clearly: she licked the wall, which was covered with yellowish, varnished boards. I felt such horror when I saw that I wished with all my heart no one would see it, but the Sisters must have found out, and quite by chance I had to cross the veranda when they were reprimanding her. The Mother Superior was shaking the girl with her phrases as if she were trying to rouse her from an attitude somewhere between sleep and scorn by giving her hell with all its horrendous torments. The Sister from our class, who was very sweet and very well-educated, was all regrets. She kept stroking her on the head and repeating: 'If only you were a clean, pretty little girl.' And the other one, the one who had no doubt turned her in, went hobbling along further up the veranda, unaware that I was behind her, swaying from one side to the other and repeating: 'So much filth in this world, so much filth in this world.'

I did not feel indifferent to the pain this word caused me. I rejected it for myself, although I believed it was appropriate for the other girl. If anyone had told me then that some time later, as I was walking in the hall in my own house, I would have to hear that said about me almost in my face, in an even lower tone, even more brazenly! Because the housekeeper said: 'So much filth in the world!' and her sarcasm seemed to suggest that if they left it up to her she'd get rid of all the filth with a quick sweep of her broom. Not the Sister: she said in *this* world, as if only the other world could be clean of it.

Why the same exclamation for such different things? Don't I understand what I'm doing? Will there ever be a time when I can understand things like other people? That would be the worst punishment I could receive. Because people live, eat, come and go as if nothing had happened, even if they see the world with disgust. Not me: if *I* ever see the world that way I'll die from it. I'd rather not live even one day more if that's where I'm headed.

But what can I be afraid of if I've made up my mind not to go anywhere, to turn back and look at everything although nothing will change?

I only went to school a few months and sometimes I get those days all mixed up. There are only a few signs to orient me: a dress I wore for the first time on a certain day but couldn't wear on another because it had gotten too short.

When everything changed was when my father came back. The days after we learned he had been wounded everyone in both houses perked up. News would be delivered to my grandmother's house; my aunt and I would go there and it seemed we all had something to do: wait for him, and then take care of him.

I expected so much from his return! I believed that he would explain things to me, that he was going to be close to me about everything I was interested in, that just by seeing him I would understand those mysteries, those dramas I knew he carried inside. But it was not like that, and it was not because he kept to himself. No, he cared for me a lot, he wanted me with him all the time, but he did not want me to ask him questions. I think my gaze and my anxiety were bad for him. He did not have the courage to remember. He hadn't gotten himself killed by the Moors, but he had gotten his memories killed by them.

He talked constantly about the ups and downs of the campaign, his suffering in the hospital, the amputation, the horrible treatments. I think the reason he talked so much was so no one else would talk, in other words, so people would only talk about what he wanted.

He had gotten used to having his old hunting dog at his feet, and he wanted everyone to listen to him like she did, without answering back. The dog would stretch out in front of him, her nose between her paws, and she would not move; all she did was turn her eyes toward him when he pointed his finger at her. Because the dog was one of the things he liked to talk about. He told everyone who came to see him the story of his poor dog, who had finally grown accustomed to the dry terrain, but she was such a delicate setter that several times after he first got her he had been afraid she would die on the dusty roads. He told how one time he managed to drag her to a puddle, how he left her there thinking she was dead, and how she caught up to him a short time later. He also talked about the jackals and imitated their howling, which he heard in the camp at night. Because the Moors would chase them with lassos and then grab them by the skin on their necks or by their tails and throw them over the barbed wire fences.

That's how he spent the winter. As long as he was convalescing he always had company and entertainment. Then he started to go out and to say he could not stand the city. He said he could not get accustomed to the climate, but I know it was something else. He said it was hard to cross the streets on crutches, that he didn't know how to do anything with his left hand, that he needed to live in a place where he could get some fresh air without having to make such an effort. Finally he decided to leave Valladolid, fix up the house we owned in Simancas, and close himself up there forever.

At the beginning of April my aunt went there with the maid; shortly afterward, my father, the housekeeper, and I went too.

We left early in the morning and arrived in about an hour. It was very hot.

In my room there was a surprise my aunt had prepared for me: a blackbird in a wicker cage. I spent a whole day doing nothing but look at it. There were some roses in a vase, some of those coarse, very fragrant roses, and every time I remember that day I seem to see the blackbird, so slender, on the rosebush that filled the house with its fragrance.

As long as that aroma lasted the novelty lasted, the trip and the move remained in the present, and we lived in that very pleasing disorder which makes time go fast and then slow in spells. Afterward I had to start getting accustomed to things because our life changed completely, although without any real reason. Of course we could no longer do the same things we did in Valladolid, but there was another, disconcerting change: I was no longer the center of the household.

Once we were in Simancas my father no longer needed any special care, but even so, the attention my aunt paid to me before he came back was never resumed.

I realized this one night as I was putting in my curlers; I began to feel tired from holding my arms over my head for so long and it dawned on me then that my aunt used to help me every night before I went to bed.

During the time my father's condition was serious I began to do it myself, because my aunt never left his side for a moment, and afterward she did not go back to helping me and I did not ask her. From that moment I began to find change in many things. I cannot say I was neglected, but I began to have a freedom I had not had before.

In Valladolid I had never gone past the front door by myself. My aunt hated living in the country; for her it was a huge sacrifice to spend much time in Simancas and she was not resigned to granting our life there any real importance. We were only to be in Simancas for a short period, so we did not take part in the life of the three or four respectable families, nor was I permitted to associate with the girls from town. She pretended she did not know what I did, as if she were telling me: you can run off if you want to; there aren't many dangers here. I did not run off, though; from time to time I found some pretext for going out — a trip to the tobacconist's to buy a pencil, or something like that — but I would be gone no longer than necessary.

I was so disoriented that at times it seemed to me I was becoming stupid. All the things I used to worry about were not interesting anymore. I no longer pestered my father with questioning looks; I didn't go back to my reading or get caught up in the fantasies I had before. When I remembered them, they seemed childish, and the truth is the things I had in my head at that time were not very important. Either I cannot remember what they were or all I thought about in those days was eating. I would jump out of bed early and station myself at the door to wait for the baker. My breakfast lasted an hour. My father had breakfast in bed and my aunt took only a sip of coffee; I would sit alone in the dining room dunking bread in my milk until I ran out of energy. Then I would go to the garden, throw a little water on the four flowerpots there and start watching the rabbits. I spent hour after dead hour listening to the faint noise rabbits make when they gnaw on cabbage stalks; that was my entertainment. The most I would think of doing sometimes was making a swing out of a rope that hung from a rafter.

About half past ten I would go back to the kitchen window to ask for bread and sausage, and I would eat it sitting on the swing. When the roosters started to crow at noon, I was already wild with hunger again.

As soon as our rooster started to crow, I realized that my stomach was what they call distressed, and it seemed to me that his song was responsible for that feeling of emptiness.

Sometimes the other roosters would start to crow in the distance; other times it would be a window in the barn whose rusty hinges squeaked in the wind with a noise so much like the crowing of a rooster that all the roosters began to sing. Our rooster was almost always on top of the trunk of a fig tree, and I would see him up there making that anxious gesture, shaking his golden crest. As he stretched his neck, a hollow would form in his chest; he would flap his wings as if he wanted to catch something with them, and those wings made me want to cry from hunger.

My aunt realized that I was getting very strong; of course she was happy, but at the same time it annoyed her to have to admit there were some advantages to the life we were leading. 'This child spends all day doing nothing; before, it was necessary to take the books from her by force, and since we've been here she's never even opened them: she's going to turn into a brute.' I would shrug my shoulders or start laughing to reassure her, but inside I thought seriously: 'I must be turning into a brute.'

Except I knew it was not the absence of books that was making me brutish, it was not that I studied before and now I did nothing but, quite clearly, that now I did nothing in a different way. Before, I worked harder at doing nothing than at anything else. To get me up there was a struggle every day, which lasted half the morning; to get me to bed at a reasonable hour, it would be the same story when they tried to tear me away from the balcony or the patio or the corner where I was playing. Because I would get furious if they interrupted me just when I was doing nothing, if they even made me shift my position without warning. This had changed, for since I had come to the village, nothing mattered to me. I got up without being called and as soon as it was dark I was ready to go to bed.

A strange thing: my aunt found it highly irritating that I was so docile, even though she had always complained about my disobedience. When someone commented on how healthy I looked, she would always say: 'Yes, she's changing every minute,' which for her was saying a lot since her favorite proverb was 'Better the devil you know than the one you don't.'

It was not because she could see into the future; it was because she was tired. If something had landed me in bed she could have sat up with me ten nights in a row. On the other hand, it wore her out to see me like that, a picture of health.

During lunch and dinner I listened with complete indifference while they talked about what to do with me. Would it be better to have me board at the Carmelite school, better to worry about my health or my education, better to bring a governess to Simancas? This last possibility was discarded even though they realized it was the most appropriate, since neither my father nor my aunt could bear to have a stranger live in the house.

It seems that in the end the most acceptable thing turned out to be having the teacher from the village give me an hour of instruction after she had finished her afternoon classes.

Everything was arranged as if we had been in the city; the teacher agreed to come to the house from five to six and a table was set up in my room with the books we had brought at the bottom of a trunk. The thought was that if things were done this way I would be able to pick up my life from Valladolid, but it was impossible. That woman seemed so strange to me! When I was little I had never felt confused in front of my professor; on the contrary, she had seemed to me the person who understood me best, and I understood her, through the gossip of my family.

I was born with that fate: to hear the people I love gossiped about. They said my professor came from a family whose fortune had fallen, that she had traveled around the world, and that she was very mannish. I was prepared to imitate everything she did, but I forgot her. No, I did not forget her; on the contrary I remembered her continually, comparing her with the other one, but finally I ended up getting interested in this one, without really liking her.

The first lessons were as agonizing for her as for me: questions and answers that petered out little by little, and, as each book was closed, the gesture that shelved it was like a sigh of relief. Then came half an hour devoted to the struggle with handwriting. She would dictate monotonously, and I wrote at top speed, finishing while you could still hear the sound of her words, which meant that my words were unintelligible and my spelling atrocious. Then the poor woman would make an effort to explain this to me, and she herself would realize that I found her explanations stupid. She would weaken, taking the pen and showing me what to do. 'If you would at least write slowly,' she would tell me. 'You have to form your letters,' and one letter after the other poured from her pen, each with the same little belly.

I did not want to discourage her, but I was prepared to keep things from going on like that. I must have tried a thousand times to start a conversation that would give me a clue to her interests or the things she could do: no luck. The poor thing hid because she knew she was not really prepared and she was afraid of making some mistake that would mean the end of her authority.

Finally, one day she arrived with a large package wrapped clumsily in newspaper, which she put on an armchair. As she was getting ready to leave, I told her I could give her some better paper, and I offered to help her wrap everything over. In the package was needlework she was taking home to prepare for the girls at her school.

That incident gave me a new perspective on my teacher, and a new world, a whole category of tasks I had never done, although they were not unknown to me. We could finally understand each other by assuming our rightful positions. I told her

20

continually that I did not know how to do any of those things, and she went on to show me each piece, feeling that she was finally a teacher of something, pulling all kinds of silly little things from the depths of her package: watch cases, pouches for carrying combs, everything worked with colored silks on padded satin.

The next day my lesson was over after ten minutes: I started talking about the needlework right away and asked my teacher to make me a list of everything I needed to order from Valladolid. This took the whole afternoon.

Then I had to argue at home for two days so they would let me go to school and do needlework with the older girls. I won on the third day: they told me I could do what I wanted so they would not have to listen to me any more, and they even sent for the materials I needed. Once again my books were forgotten.

I was neither modest nor hardworking, and I did not go out of my way to learn, but I never felt comfortable with people until I got them talking about something they knew better than I did; otherwise, they seemed superficial to me. What they did made no difference to me, even if I would never have to do it myself. I might watch the carpenter plane a board, or watch the butcher wield his knife as he severed the meat from the bone: when they worked with true mastery it gave me a feeling of admiration and well-being that I could only express by saying, 'That's how God meant things to be done.' When I found out that my teacher could do such beautiful work, I finally had something to talk with her about. I asked her about all the different kinds of needlework I had seen my aunts do and she knew all of them. There, in my grandmother's house, in that dreadful room where the things they talked about were never clear and always malicious, the frames and little baskets seemed silly and boring. Sometimes I would look over the shoulder of one of my aunts and what I saw held no secret for me: I was as skilled as any one of them, but I had no interest in proving it. On the other hand, I liked to let my teacher show me; I liked to watch her start things and complete them, to watch her join the stitches, shading them with colored silks, and to watch her taper the raised areas in her white work. I especially admired the way she did that. Where did she get the delicacy it took to tighten the tiny waists of those raised areas curving in the initials of English Roundhand she put on handkerchiefs, or in the flowers, where one half of the leaf was embossed and the other shaded? First she would prepare a padding of rather wide stitches and then she would cover it slowly, stitching from side to side with satiny cotton thread. She would start the crescents by making them plump toward the center and flat at the ends; then she would polish them with her ivory stiletto. She trimmed them so lovingly! When she finished they were like little pearls, like candies; in the sun their whiteness was blinding, they were so shiny.

I spent months enraptured like that; it's incredible, but I did.

Vacation arrived and only two girls who were much older still went to the teacher's house with me in the afternoons, to embroider with her in the garden, under the grape arbor. We hardly talked: the hoopoes would walk along the top of the mud wall as if no one were there. When we finished our work we ate grapes and bread the teacher gave us in exchange for our company. Then those two girls and I would go down to the threshing floors next to the river, and we would sit there on a pile of straw until it started to get dark.

One of them always sat down on either side of me and then they said they could not talk about certain things because I was too little. 'Don't be stupid,' I told them. 'Talk about whatever you want.' They always ended up talking about things they said were naughty. Sometimes what they said interested me, sometimes it was boring, because they repeated the same things a hundred times; then I would let myself fall back in the straw and watch the stars come out.

School started the first of September and everything was so normal at the beginning it seemed nothing would ever change; toward the middle of the month it did, though, simply from a change in the weather. There was a furious rash of storms. In the mornings, nothing unusual would happen, but after noon the sky over Valladolid would begin to get gray and the cloud would advance little by little across the valley; then another cloud would appear from behind the hill, and when they met over Simancas it seemed that not a single stone would be left where it was.

In class you could begin to feel the storm in the restlessness of the girls. The teacher would rap on the desk with her ruler, shouting violently to make them be quiet and getting herself as worked up as everyone else, until we could hear the thunder starting, still distant but clear enough to erase the sense of discord. Then we would blame it all on the storm, light the stub of the votive candle blessed during Holy Week, and pray while the thunderclaps grew louder and louder until they exploded over our heads.

After one or two of those raindrops that sound like tin, great big ones would begin to hit the windowpanes at an angle; you could see the first ones shoot past like arrows, but they quickly turned into a thick curtain.

The girls crowded at the windows to watch the streams forming outside the school and there was no way to calm them down. The teacher was overwhelmed; putting her hands on her head, she turned to me suddenly and said: 'Leticia, tell them a story.' Before I could answer, she began to scream at the girls: 'Quiet, children, Leticia's going to tell a story! Quiet children! . . .' She shouted that ten times.

When there was absolute silence, I told a story and then I

told another and after that another; we spent the afternoon like that until the streams had shrunk enough to fit into the gutters and we could go out. The next day the same thing happened again, step by step, and when the teacher shouted, 'Quiet, children, Leticia's going to tell a story,' there was a new ruckus because some of them wanted the same ones as the day before and some wanted new ones. Then one of the older girls whispered something into the teacher's ear. Without waiting at all, 'Quiet, children,' she screamed, striking the desk with her ruler. 'Leticia's going to sing!'

This silenced them even better and until the beginning of October the same sequence of events occurred every afternoon: first there was fighting, then there was praying, then there was singing.

Once the storms were over, the afternoon work was taken seriously again and I was again in my little chair beside the teacher, on the platform.

One day when the whispering of the girls was not too loud, the teacher said to me:

'You know what I'm thinking, Leticia? You should study music. You have such a good ear!'

'That would be wonderful,' I exclaimed. 'But where can I study music here?'

'We'll see; I know a woman who has given lessons to other children. She's the archivist's wife. I'll take you to see her; ask your father for permission.'

When one of these situations came up I realized that the atmosphere in my house was more charged every day. Any proposal, any innovation I tried to make raised a storm of discontent. All it took was a simple request like that and the looks they gave me seemed to say, 'How could you think of such a thing? What will you want next? . . .' It was not that my ideas seemed wrong to them; I could see that my aunt in particular was hard put to find any reason for opposing me. Her anguished looks would start as soon as I started to speak, before she knew what I was going to say. 'Do what you want,' she would tell me as I finished, completely overwhelmed. 'Do what your aunt tells you,' my father would say between his teeth.

I could not understand what was wrong with them. It was clear that, from egotism, they wanted nothing to do with people who did not interest them, who might stop by at any moment on inopportune visits; but their unhappiness with me was also evident. Continually I had to hear complaints about how I had abandoned my studies and predictions about how I would end up acquiring the habits of the bumpkins I associated with. Underneath all this there was something like a presentiment of misfortune that I found irritating. I was so serene, so sure of myself; but when I started to think about their fears I felt a kind of absence in my head, as if I were about to faint. Finally I would shake off that dizziness and end up doing what I wanted.

My musical apprenticeship could hardly have been shorter. Thursday afternoon the teacher took me to doña Luisa's house where I was offered everything I could want, although not right then. A boy of three or four was tugging at doña Luisa's skirt, and in her arms there was another little one, just a few months old. She told us that in fact the year before she had prepared some little girls for their solfeggio exam at the conservatory, but that after her baby was born she couldn't keep up with so much work. She would be nursing for another few months, and after that she could start again. She also told me that in the meantime, since she couldn't get through the day without opening the piano for at least half an hour, she had organized a group of girls who came in the late afternoon for instruction in choruses and novenas for the church, and that I could sing with them to start, to get used to it. I will always remember that when we said goodbye at the door, she told me, 'Now you know that starting tomorrow you can come about six. Well, *you* can come at any time; goodbye, dear.'

When I heard her say 'goodbye, dear,' I knew she was not really Castilian. Her assurance dazzled me. She was not elegant like some of the women I admired in Valladolid; I don't know if this word can be used here, but she was *worldly*. I know that I'm using this word in a way it's not usually used: to me, worldly means that she does not insist on being still all the time the way everyone in my family does. Neither did she seem like a traveler, like my first professor. Well, that one was a princess; but there was something enterprising about her. She was wearing a thin voile dress that was coming unfastened everywhere and she had on some mules of red morocco leather that made her ankles look even bonier.

That was my first impression when I looked at her at the door of her house as I was leaving. Around her large gray eyes there were dark rings, between blue and green. Just because of those eyes you could say she was very pretty, and in truth she was. She looked disheveled, in an appealing sort of way, and she was so thin it seemed that instead of nursing one baby she must have been nursing ten all at the same time.

Her gaze seemed so frank, so open, as she said goodbye to us that afternoon. Later I began to see that her face was always identical; there were only a few serious occasions when she could change her expression, when that same frankness would get hard, and her voice, which was usually very smooth, would turn into a shriek. It was a side of her I never saw for more than a few fleeting moments, but now I am sure she has become like that forever. Her confident gaze is something she will never have again. At least I know her gaze has disappeared; the house, on the other hand, is probably the same. How can that be possible! Before, before everything that happened, had it also been the same then? If I think about these things I end up losing faith. This solitude is driving me crazy: the fact that I'm here with my despair and other people are in some other place with theirs, and at the same time things stay the way they were. Because then I think: that light from other times, that atmosphere, they were meaningless, they were not made for me.

I knew that house from passing by on the street. Its dark stone facade had caught my attention. On each side of the front door there were just two windows with grates; upstairs there were four, joined by a continuous balcony with gold balls on the corners of the railing. Under the eaves there was only a very simple cornice. But the front door . . . the impression the light from that doorway made on me as I approached was never erased, not even by the habit of walking through it every day, as I did eventually. The entryway was a square vestibule, but what made it specially inviting was a very wide hall with an arched ceiling that opened from the far side and spanned the house. At the end there was a glass-enclosed sun porch completely covered by a grape vine, and from the dark street the hallway looked like a tunnel filled with green light. When I used to walk by, before I knew I would ever enter that house, it made me think of the entrance to paradise. I always walked by slowly so I could gaze into it, so we could gaze at each other, because it seemed to be gazing at me like an eye.

The next day I went before six: I could not wait any longer. Doña Luisa set about taking me through the house right away, before I could express an interest in it, but she told me she wanted me to know how they did things. 'See,' she told me, 'downstairs here, on the left side, there are only two rooms, one facing the street and the other facing the garden; they are both set aside for my husband, otherwise the children won't let him read.' She opened the door to the second room halfway and I saw there was a desk covered with books and a sofa with two large leather armchairs. She continued the tour: on the right side, in the front, was the parlor, and in the back, the dining room and kitchen. The sun porch extended across the first floor from one side to the other, but they had divided it with a screen to keep kitchen odors from traveling to the left side of the house.

'Now you're going to see my den,' doña Luisa told me. We went up a stone stairway that seemed to be embedded in one side of the vestibule, and upstairs, where the back part was divided the same as below, she showed me her room with two cribs for the children on the right; on the left there was a room that had everything you could think of: wardrobes, clothes racks, bathtubs. The maids' room was in the attic.

As she opened the door in the center of the landing at the top of the stairs, she told me: 'This is the piano room.' I ran my eyes around it. 'It's beautiful,' I said with all my heart.

No one would have suspected what that room was like. It was huge; it extended across the whole front of the house, across the four windows, and it was completely empty, naked: not a chair, not a curtain, not even a nail on the wall. Nothing but the grand piano, with its bench, in the right-hand corner. The remains of a hanger for holding the chandelier still dangled from a beam in the middle of the ceiling, but its iron hook was broken and the cord had been gathered up and tied into a ball over the transom.

I had said those words and she saw that I meant them. Besides, she would never have doubted it, because that's how the room looked to her too. We stood there without saying anything, without knowing what else to say. I was leaning against the wall, with my arms crossed. She was trying to keep the children from fussing, as always. Then I got the baby to leave his mother's arms and come to mine, and she could stretch a bit. She fluffed out her dress and managed to free her skirt from the hands of the other child; she looked like a little girl.

Suddenly we heard footsteps down in the entryway and doña

Luisa leaned over the stairway calling, 'Is that you, girls? Come on upstairs.'

Up came two girls I already knew. The nursemaid was behind them, bringing a box of matches; she took the children by the hand and led them toward the landing.

Doña Luisa lit the candles on the piano, placed some papers on the music stand and sat down. 'The *Salve*,' she said. After a few chords, the girls began to sing, but before too long doña Luisa stopped playing. They weren't fitting the words with the music very well; of course, they were singing without understanding what they sang. She did not try to explain it to them, all she did was teach the girls how much time to give each syllable. They started over, and when they were at about the middle, I began to hear footsteps coming up behind me on tiptoe. 'What vocation, girls, what vocation,' doña Luisa said without stopping. The four girls who had just arrived went to stand beside the others and found their way into the singing as best they could.

My life was divided between school and that house; I don't know where the mornings went. As soon as I had picked up the needlework frame and sat beside the teacher, I would start to tell her what had happened the day before at doña Luisa's. I would always arrive there at a few minutes past five, the minutes it took me to run from school as fast as I could; and until the other girls got there I helped doña Luisa with the thousand things she had to do, usually with the cooking. She left things at a point where she could finish them after the music lesson. Her cook was terrible, whereas she herself made wonderful Catalonian dishes. When I described them to the teacher, she tried them at home and told me the next day how they turned out so I could ask doña Luisa about things that went wrong.

But we did more in the kitchen than just chores; we nibbled constantly. I had never ever done that at home, and she taught me how. No matter what it was, we tried it, even things that one would never think of eating between meals. When she made those white beans with pork loin and parsley, she always made a little more than could fit in the pan and we would eat it between the two of us with two teaspoons. She picked out the pieces of meat and gave them all to me; and when she stuffed the turnovers, as she put a piece of pine nut, an olive, and a raisin in each one, she fed bits to me and her little boy, who would stand by the table with his mouth open like a baby sparrow. Afterward, when she was heating the oil, she fried crusts of bread for the maids.

Sometimes the cook scolded her, because she said she nibbled so much in the kitchen she could not eat at the table, and that's why she was so thin. She would look at the cook, opening her eyes wide without either laughing or looking serious. 'Well, that's true, you're right,' she would say, but she kept on doing the same thing.

Sometimes her pupils had to wait when they came for singing lessons because she was in the middle of doing something she could not leave. Other times she would spend so long with them there was nothing ready when it was time for dinner. Then she would be upset and go round in circles looking for someone to blame.

One of the days when we had sung the most, everything from springtime hymns to the Virgin to Christmas carols, we were still in the doorway, all of us standing in a circle around doña Luisa and making plans about what we would sing, when doña Luisa's husband appeared at the door. The doctor was with him, and doña Luisa pressed forward to greet him, hunting for excuses that would explain her unkempt appearance. 'You know, doctor, these girls are driving me crazy,' she said, putting her hands on the doctor's shoulders. She was looking at her husband, though, and I could tell she wanted to ask him: What time is it?

He smiled when he heard her and looked at our group, shaking his head. Suddenly he reached out a hand and grabbed all my curls, pinning them in a fistful at the back of my neck. 'This is the one who must give you the most trouble,' he said. 'With this hair, she's bound to be something.'

The girls had slipped gradually between the adults and the door and disappeared; doña Luisa repeated a few formalities to the doctor and went to the kitchen; the hand holding my hair had let go of it all except for one ringlet that was still between its fingers. I looked at those two men who kept talking without paying any attention to me and I looked at the end of my curl still caught in that hand, which was rubbing it like a hand judging the quality of a piece of cloth, without realizing that the curl was connected to my temple.

By pulling furtively, I managed to get it loose; I said a brief good-night and started to run.

I ran as if someone were after me and I had a very strange feeling; I did not know if it was because I had behaved foolishly or because of how they had behaved toward me. Also I was worried about doña Luisa. I looked at the clock as I passed a store; it said nine. I was afraid she might have had an argument with her husband: he had impressed me as a highly temperamental man and a very unlikable one.

It was not the first time I had seen him. The month before, when we were still having that rash of storms, I was walking near the castle with another girl and we stopped for no particular reason to watch some large drops of water falling from a gutter into the moat. He came out just then, crossed the bridge, and passed right beside us. He was wearing a brown raincoat with the hood up and a white silk scarf around his neck. 'That's the archivist,' said the girl who was with me.

'He looks like a Moorish king,' I answered.

When I got home, totally absorbed in that memory, there

was a tragedy waiting for me too because I was so late, but it was a tragedy of silences, and precisely at that moment I had a stroke of intuition and I understood what was going on in my house.

I was more wound up than usual, more perceptive, and it seemed to me that I could see everything clearly; I turned their silence into a watchtower.

When my father went to his room, I asked my aunt: 'Who came this afternoon?'

'No one,' she answered mechanically.

Suddenly she looked at me, though, and saw there was an ulterior motive in my question.

'I don't know,' she said, correcting herself. 'I went out for a while, so I don't know who might have come.'

While I was watching her, she had watched me: I realized that I would get nothing that way and I decided to try a different tack for coming up with my proof. I went to bed prepared to put all my energy into it the next day, but the next day I could not come up with the necessary resolution. I had not forgotten and I did not think proof would be too difficult: the fact is that the warmth, all the transcendence it had for me the night before had disappeared. In the morning I saw it as something probable, but not certain, and above all, like something that had to be proved all by itself, although I did not stop thinking that I should not neglect it. Nevertheless, the routine things I enjoyed doing were more pressing and I got completely caught up in them again.

At doña Luisa's house I did not find the least trace of a storm; on the contrary, she was waiting for me impatiently, with a still unopened package that had just been delivered by the carrier. We immediately undid it together, extracting a whole raft of screws, screwdrivers, hammers, yards of cord, and porcelain insulators.

That was during the time we were involved in a huge project

of fixing up the house, and we had decided to begin with the electricity. We changed the broken switches and put plugs for portable lamps in every room; on the piano we put artificial candles with electric light bulbs.

The project was so large that many days I had to miss school and some days I would also slip over there for a while in the morning. The straw matting in the parlor was pulled up so the floor could be waxed, because all the changes were occasioned by the arrival of the furniture they had left in Seville when they moved; it had finally been sent for and was now at the station in Valladolid.

The day the furniture came, the two of us were there waiting at nine in the morning. They opened the doors all the way, and the men who delivered it were in and out all over the place.

The only important items were four enormous crates of books that were placed in an abandoned dovecote in the middle of the garden. The rest were several pieces of antique furniture the men set about uncrating, and when they had the job about half finished, doña Luisa called the cook and told her:

'Go take those men a nice glass of wine.'

She held her hands some distance apart, as if to indicate the large glasses. The girl watched the men drinking, and she said:

'It's just as well they won't be coming back here, otherwise you'd have them craving sweets all the time too.'

Doña Luisa nodded her head as if it were undeniable.

We spent a whole week arranging the parlor, which turned out perfectly.

We hung a large mirror over a console table and just a few other things on the walls: two cornucopias and some small family portraits. The chairs were that kind with an oval back. In front of the sofa, a small lacquered pedestal table, and on the last day, the curtains, which doña Luisa had made herself from plain white voile; they were gathered at the top but loose below.

Just when I thought everything was finished, I saw her bringing an enormous demijohn filled with water, which she put on the floor in front of the balcony. Then she went to the garden, cut a stalk of hollyhocks, and put it in the neck of the large wickered bottle. At that moment I saw her again as she had been the day I met her and I remembered how I had described her. Once again I saw that quality of hers I called *worldly*, and which was nothing other than a perfect ease about everything in the world.

The work was finished and the two of us stood in the doorway a while watching how the light passed through the curtains, sparkled on the water in the demijohn, and spread over the waxed surface of the floor, along the backs of the chairs and the cornucopias.

I was enraptured and would have liked to express my admiration, and I turned to look at her so as to say something. She was looking at me also and she also felt the need to make some remark; she took me by the arm then, telling me: 'Today I'm going to make a timbale for supper.'

We went out of the room, closing the door and warning the maids and the children not to walk on the waxed floor.

In the last days of November, on some of the afternoons when it was sunny, as soon as dinner was over I would take a walk with doña Luisa instead of going to school. We would go down to sit on the pilings that jutted into the river on the right-hand side of the bridge and we would stay there for a long time, looking silently at the bare birches on the islands. As we walked back the sound of water swirling around stones would still be in our ears.

At other times we went out with the nursemaid and the children; then we would walk down the other side to the outskirts of town as far as the church of the Arrabal, where we always went in to pray for a while. And what was bound to happen happened.

One afternoon, at the door of the chapel, we met up with my Aunt Aurelia.

Doña Luisa greeted her immediately as if she had known her all her life, and my aunt, half embarrassed and half annoyed, began to rack her brain in search of excuses for never having visited doña Luisa. She thanked her more than a hundred times for everything she had done for me and she described the care my father required in the most exaggerated way imaginable, using it as a reason for leading such a secluded life.

Doña Luisa found those whiny excuses depressing, and she tried to stop my aunt and reassure her with her own openness. 'I have nothing to forgive you for,' she repeated. 'Leticia is my best friend and I'm delighted to have her company at any time,' she said, trying with all her might to draw my aunt into a more cheerful and natural conversation. But this was impossible with my aunt. She realized it was necessary to change the subject and immediately came up with another, the only one that would allow her to continue hammering on her complaint: the worry my education was causing her. With this she managed to be listened to, but she did not count on doña Luisa's enterprising nature, which immediately led her to look for a solution and prompted her, since for the moment she could not find one, to try to win my aunt's confidence by telling her about numerous instances in which she had helped to resolve similar situations.

Doña Luisa was talking about private schools, public high schools, innumerable courses of study. My aunt was talking about education as in upbringing. I know exactly what she meant. But since the real issue was her determination to complain about something, and she could not complain about my manners since my behavior was irreproachable in every way, she found herself forced to speak of my neglected books, to go on about the care they had lavished on my schooling and about how sad it was to see that I let everything go so quickly.

It was almost impossible to see an idea through those gray eyes I knew so well, but at least I had discovered something of how they worked: when they remained fixed for a few seconds on a given point, it was because something had passed behind them, and that something always came out half an hour later, in one way or another.

Doña Luisa suggested to my aunt that they take the shortcut on the way back up so as to catch the last rays of sun on the road above. While we were walking up, 'You're right,' she repeated as if she were following the thread of my aunt's conversation. 'It's really a shame, with the talent this child has.'

She had never praised me; I had never spoken with her about anything except trivialities. Why did she suddenly come out with something about my talent?

It seemed strange and it impressed me a lot. I never paid attention to praise, yet that time I would have liked to stop the conversation there, to make her explain why she said what she did; but I could not do it in front of my aunt.

In my imagination I started to work out a plan to engage her in a similar conversation when we were by ourselves.

I was absorbed in that, looking at the ground, when I heard her say: 'Look, here comes my husband with the doctor; they walk together every afternoon, when he leaves the Archive.'

There were greetings, introductions, stupid, meaningless questions, when suddenly doña Luisa decided to start up again with the topic from a little while before: 'Miss Valle was just saying to me . . .' I started to stare at the sky.

I don't know how long that lasted, and I don't remember what they said. My aunt continued to complain, since she found her opinions seconded; doña Luisa continued to offer suggestions. 'We were always very fond of teaching,' she repeated like a chorus.

At one moment when my aunt was speaking with the doctor,

36

I saw that she was asking her husband in a low voice: '*You'd* have time now, wouldn't you?' He shook his head in a way that meant neither yes nor no.

The two men resumed their walk. We kept on toward town.

I do not remember how the afternoon ended, but I do remember that I lost my tranquillity. There was a threat hanging over me, and the most terrible thing about it was how it never quite burst.

Every day, when I went to doña Luisa's house, I intended to remain absolutely silent about those issues. I told myself that if I didn't, all the plans she might have come up with in a moment of excitement would fade into oblivion; later, when it turned out that in fact I was right, I felt an anxiety and an uneasiness that seized my imagination and kept me from thinking about anything else. I even caught myself trying to talk about schooling, uttering sentences that might recall the conversation of that afternoon, and when I finally doubted she had even the least ability to remember anything at all, one day, right out of the blue she said to me:

'I'll tell you that what your aunt said is absolutely true; you have a head made for books.'

I waited for her to continue, but she did not. She took my silence as a period and started to talk about something else.

We were in the kitchen; at that moment, as we were starting to cut the pasta dough we had just made, I heard her say:

'Well! What's happened to bring you at this hour?'

I raised my head and realized she was not talking to me; the master of the house had entered like a shadow and was leaning against the doorway watching us.

Instead of answering, he asked: 'Does my pupil also help you in the kitchen?'

And she replied, as if the conversation had begun a while before, as if everyone had already made some agreement:

'She has already learned everything I taught her; we'll see how soon you can say the same.'

There was a silence and I assured myself they were joking. Smiling, with a smile I don't know how I managed, I looked first at her and then at him, and he said to me, motioning with his head, 'Come on, I'm going to give you a test.'

I stood there paralyzed; he stepped back as if to let me walk through the door, and without wondering if I would, he added: 'Let's see that talent.'

I refused to look at him again; it seemed to me that he could have told from my eyes how angry I felt. I could fill hundreds of pages with the things I thought on my way from the kitchen to the study; I aged ten years in that moment. I looked so small to myself that it made me feel sorry for that self, as only adults can feel sorry for small children.

There was nothing I dreaded more than a test. Even at the times I was used to studying, a test had seemed hateful to me, because I knew that I would never manage to pull the right thing at the right moment from the confusion in my head, and that suddenly I was falling like a rabbit into a trap, because I had been leading a totally stupid life for almost a year.

We went in through the door off the hall and he had me sit next to the desk facing the large door with glass panes that led to the sun porch; he stood with his back to the light and I realized I would fall into a daze if I kept looking through the leaves in the arbor at the sun shining in the garden. To prevent that, and especially to keep him from seeing that I was about to burst into tears, I started to look offhandedly at the things on his desk. 'Do you like the monkey?' he asked me. I had not been paying attention to anything in particular, but suddenly a monkey's head the size of a coconut leapt to my eye; it was extremely lifelike and expressive, and it wore a sort of Turkish cap.

'It looks like bronze, but it's fired clay,' he said, sliding it closer to me across the desk. He took off its cap, which was like a lid, so I could see the head was filled with cigars. Afterward he put the monkey back in its place, caressing its face and changing its position several times until he was looking at it from the perspective he liked best. Then he began to tell me how the monkey was a gift from a friend who bought it in Paris at the Exposition of 1900, how it had been given to him more than ten years before, and how he could never move it from his desk, partly because he was fond of it, partly because that exposition represented a page in history.

He looked at me to see if I understood.

'You know?' he said. 'The world was like a world from Jules Verne then.'

I jumped in my chair, although I hid it by crossing one leg over the other. All of my anxiety disappeared as if by magic and I began listening to him.

He talked for more than an hour and a half; I would never be able to repeat what he said; I can only say that the things he named came alive in the room.

I saw Ataulf ride by on his horse, I saw Jacob's ladder and the guillotine from the French Revolution. Finally he brought me back to reality by saying:

'It seems like you're the one who's giving me a test. I talk and talk, letting you sit there and not say a word instead of making *you* recite the events of our glorious history for *me*.'

My terror must have been written on my face, because he held out a hand as if to restrain me.

'Don't exert yourself,' he said, 'the truth is I never thought you knew so much.'

Since I had not opened my mouth, I thought he was starting to make fun of me and everything looked gloomy again. I exerted an immense effort to regain my serenity, and finally I could begin to say:

'I swear that at one time I studied quite a bit, it's just that . . .'

He interrupted me:

'What do you think I've been doing, silly? Telling you stories? Hardly: I realized right away that with you it would have been useless to start out with questions; on the other hand, while I've been talking it has been very easy for me to see on your face what you understood and what you didn't.'

Once again I felt as though I had fallen into a mousetrap; this time it did not bother me anymore and I laughed so hard I almost cried. We went out into the hallway, and I went over to the door into the dining room.

'Goodbye,' I shouted. 'I have to run because it's so late.'

I reached home without my feet touching the ground and I saw it was not late. They were starting to get preparations under way for supper, but they were in no particular hurry. I did not know what to do with myself, because I could not be still, and I decided to go outside near the front door, telling them to call me when it was time to eat.

It was cold; our street was narrow and dark; and on the corner there was a single bulb with a white reflector, which swung back and forth endlessly. I leaned against the doorway, turning my back to the light, so I could see only the unlighted part of the street. The cold, which I usually detest, felt pleasant as it brushed my forehead, like when you splash cologne on your face; by looking at the darkness I managed not to think about anything.

An hour later I was in bed, shivering and trying to see clearly everything that had happened.

At first, as always, what I felt was wild happiness because events that had terrified me in the beginning had turned out so well, and also satisfaction, a savoring of everything I had heard down to the smallest detail. This was what I called being in my element: having something to admire. I had only experienced a similar state a few times, as I was leaving the theater; what I felt then was so intense they never wanted to take me because they said I got drunk on what I saw. Only this was not like the theater: a set scene, which you cannot enter and one that cannot be prolonged after it's over. This, on the other hand, had only just gotten started and within me I knew how to keep it going.

I thought immediately about gathering up all my old books, which I had agreed to take the next day to see if we could use them, and although I was sure my new professor would never ask me those blunt questions they ask when they want to prove that you don't know and never did know anything, I myself wanted to subject my memory to a test like that. I set out to review everything I knew, as if I were setting out to count the money in my pocket.

I remembered having done this before. At the times when I was studying a lot, some days such an intense reaction would get started in my head that there would be no way to stop it. One question would lead me to others and I would hear the dining room clock strike one and then two without being able to fall asleep. In my memory I would go over all my books, from the first one I ever read in my life up to the last, and I would recall the sentences exactly as they were placed on the page, with any small printer's errors there had been and the marks I had made in pencil. Then I would go over all the verse I knew by heart: the rhymed fables, the songs, and, finally, the prayers. Between the time I was seven and nine I used to do this often, until I would work myself into a fever. Well, that night I tried to do the same thing and mentally I went over the first pages of my World History. Very quickly, without any detail, without any warmth, I reviewed the facts about the ancient civilizations, up to the Middle Ages. I started to think about the first Crusade, following the text of my book precisely, and when I said, 'The second half, formed by knights led by Godfrey de Bouillon . . . ,' I remembered how in the afternoon, as he said just that name, my professor had picked up a pencil that was lying on the folder. He did it without thinking and he kept his hands on the desk while he spoke, moving that pencil with his fingertips. Depending on what he was talking about, the pencil resembled a spear, a cross, or a banner.

This was not my delirium, it was actual reality, and studying it again as it appeared in my memory, I forgot the exercise I had set out for myself. When I realized what had happened, I took up that exercise again as best I could, but it erased itself on me a hundred times more, because the same kind of memories continued to hound me.

Each time I regained consciousness I told myself that the enchantment of the afternoon had been so strong I would not be able to erase its impression easily, but to myself I never lie; I immediately discarded that idea and saw the truth of the matter clearly. What was happening to me was that I was beginning to suffer the consequences of having become so brutish.

Laziness had become so habitual for me I could no longer throw myself into that activity from before: now I slid into a kind of daydream. I gave in to thoughts about things that wrapped me in their charm, their warmth . . . It was a new sensation for me, but at the same time it was undoubtedly the result of the life I'd been leading.

That's how far I had plunged into the world of women, 'with their silliness and their petty vices,' to use my confessor's phrase. When he scolded me for indulging my sweet tooth he always told me the story of Saint Monica, which he repeated in order to accustom me to not drink water, so that later I would be able to not drink wine.

I had never seen much point to the story, but that night I thought I understood it was about getting used to making a small effort so as gradually to be capable of a larger one, and the weakness that overcame me when I tried to concentrate on my studies seemed to confirm its meaning precisely. The disgust I felt then at being a woman took my faith away so hard I could have cried.

Once again, like the moment when I steeled myself to submit to that test, I looked at myself with unspeakable pity and distance.

I realized at the time that a new phase of my life was beginning there; at that moment I acquired something like a new faculty, which began to develop immediately, because by night it was already different and much more complicated. The truth is, I also felt sorry for myself, but at the same time I looked at myself so cruelly!

I seemed totally ridiculous with all my unfounded pretensions. Brutish, that more than anything; I was nothing but a brute and I had no grace whatsoever, not one bit of character.

I was great for sitting there beside the teacher with my mass of ringlets falling over the embroidery and my arms like spider's claws pulling the thread, but in that study where what happened was different from anything I had ever experienced . . . pupils, yes, of course, but boys; barbarians if you will, but not this, not what I was.

What had become of those dreams I nourished when I studied with my first professor? Each time we had a lesson I would note her tailored suit, her simplicity, her masculine style and I would think: when I'm like her . . . and just when I found myself in a situation better than one I ever dreamed possible, it turned out I was a girl like all the rest. Not even that, I was no more than the perfect Miss Know-it-all.

Those passions tossed and turned in me so much my throat ached as if I were struggling to swallow them and they kept me awake in a way I could never manage when I wanted to think about my books.

It was dawn before I fell asleep, but even so I leapt out of bed at eight; I was convinced that even an entire morning would never give me enough time for all the preparations I planned, which in the end were nothing more than collecting my books and notebooks, sharpening a pencil, and putting a new point in my pen.

Once that was done, I got dressed, and I did not put the white pinafore on over my dress as usual because I decided to go to school only long enough to tell the teacher about my new arrangements for studying and to say goodbye. I put on a red and blue Scotch plaid dress, because it was the darkest one I had and because I had once heard my former professor praise Scotch fabrics.

As soon as dinner was over, I went to my room to get everything and leave, but suddenly I remembered something and went back to the dining room. My aunt was there getting the tray with coffee and cognac ready to take to my father in his room. I started to talk with her, pretending that I felt calm, as if I were there because I had nothing else to do. At the moment she lifted the tray from the table, I took it from her hands without interrupting what I was telling her, and we went into my father's room together. I put the things on the small table next to his armchair and immediately spoke of something that might interest him. 'Every day,' I told him, 'I plan to pass by the tobacconist's to buy you some brushes for your pipes and I always forget; today I'll remember for sure. Do you still have one that draws?'

My father showed me the one he had in his hand. I promised him that the next day I would clean them all. I looked quickly at the others, touched all the objects on the table, finally gave my father a kiss, and left.

My heart was pounding like a spy's heart must pound. I had been planning that for days, but I had lacked the nerve to do it. Well, now it's done, I told myself.

44

I ran to school; well, no, I did not run, because I did not dare to run without my white pinafore. But I got there in a hurry. No one had sat down yet.

My arrival was enough to disrupt the afternoon, because the teacher herself said:

'I know already, I already know what you've come to tell me; since yesterday morning I've known that you're going to have classes with don Daniel.'

'Then you knew even before I did,' I said. And I told her briefly what my first lesson had been like. Of course I told her about it in the special way I told her things, very superficially and as if in jest, emphasizing the comical aspect of the fear it had caused me.

She was happy, because even though she regretted my defection from the school, after all, she had been the one who took me to that house.

She made me promise a thousand times that I would return from time to time, and the girls gave me a noisy goodbye with shouts and hugs.

When I was just about to leave, a girl a little taller than I came up to me and I thought she was going to give me another hug, but she looked me over from head to toe, put one arm around my waist and made me dance a few steps with her.

I got away in a hurry, and when I was walking up the street I realized that what she did had not been a criticism but a comment on my dress. The girl had not meant me any harm, but she was one of the ones who notice everything and she had done it as if to say: 'What a tiny waist!'

At once I began to imagine myself as I would be in five minutes in front of that imposing desk with my big head and my tiny waist: like an insect, as ridiculous as one of those ants you see running around everywhere.

I felt so upset I paused to turn a corner and go home to

change my clothes, but it was too late and I started to walk again, thinking: Why exaggerate everything so much? What had made me decide to change my outfit that day, when I could have gone the way I always did, without putting that worry in my head? And I had told the teacher I couldn't go to embroider with her anymore because I needed all my time to study.

This was not true because it was enough if I studied in the mornings. The real reason I decided to stop going was so I could get away from those womanly activities, but then even at the moment I was thinking clearly enough to make that decision I could not keep myself from putting on a nice little dress for the occasion.

Well, the fact was I had broken with the teacher. On the other hand, I was going to be seeing doña Luisa more every day, and that relationship was much more engrossing than the other. Would I be able to change it, or would she herself understand? After all, she was the one who had decided my life would change as if by royal decree.

When I got to her house, it seemed to me that she was definitely inclined in the right direction. As soon as she saw me with my satchel full of books she took off her apron, made me put the books on the dining room table, and buried her nose in them. She opened the geography book and began hunting for something. When I got tired of waiting and was about to ask her what she was reading, she closed the book and said to me:

'I was looking at the place occupied by Mediterranean Spain in the production of silk.'

That struck me as an odd thing to be interested in! But I did not say anything. She picked up a few books with one hand and told me to bring the rest and get myself settled in the study; I could work there without being bothered.

Behind us, my professor entered with his imperceptible footsteps. 'You see, she was not wasting time,' doña Luisa said to him, and she left immediately. He looked through my books in a minute and discounted all of them. I needed to send to Valladolid for the books they used at the high school, he said, beginning to make a list.

Before he could finish, doña Luisa appeared at the door.

'I'm only interrupting because I know you haven't gotten down to work yet,' she said.

She stayed for a while without saying anything, leaning on the edge of the desk. Her hands were so long and slender they allowed the movement of the tendons to show beneath the skin; around her nails there were bits of dough. She began to pick them off, using the nails on one hand to clean those of the other while she spoke:

'When you come tomorrow, before you start to work, we have to measure for the shelves in this study; by now the books outside in the dovecote are probably being eaten by mice.'

When he had finished the list, although he had said nothing while doña Luisa spoke about the shelves, my professor glanced around the room and said:

'I'm terrified to think of having to start arranging those books some day.'

I sensed it was the last statement of the afternoon. There had been nothing but preparations. 'See you tomorrow,' I said and left.

As I got close to home, I remembered I had planned to go in through the back door that day, but everything had languished so much in the afternoon and my spirits were so dampened that I asked myself: What for? and walked home the same way as always. Just at the last minute, I thought: It's despicable to falter like this. I turned the corner and went through the garden to the back door.

In the kitchen, the housekeeper and the maid did not look surprised to see me; I went over to the fire to warm my hands.

'Did the doctor come today?' I asked them without warning.

'No, why?' the housekeeper answered sourly, as usual.

'No reason,' I answered. 'My throat hurts a little, and it would be nice,' I added, 'if he came more often so my father didn't have to spend the afternoons by himself.'

There was no reply. As I got ready to leave, I said again: 'No one came today either?'

'No one,' the housekeeper said.

I went to the dining room. My aunt was not there. I opened the sideboard and checked the mark I had made on the cognac label. The bottle had just been opened when I poured the glass and now it was two-thirds empty.

That night at the table, watching now with complete certainty, I could measure the dimensions of evil, the havoc it had caused and the havoc it could cause.

At first I felt so overwhelmed I didn't dare lift my eyes from my plate, but I heard the symptom that had occasioned my suspicion. In truth, it was the only symptom: when my father spoke, he pronounced his words very poorly. What he said made perfect sense, but he had trouble with his *r*'s in particular. Sometimes he would repeat a word and he could not get it to come out any better the second time than the first.

I thought: It will probably stop here, it's no doubt a habit he picked up in the war and he'll be strong enough not to let it get worse. I accepted this, since it did not occur to me to ask even at the bottom of my heart for it to get better. I realized that it was like an artificial fog he was building up around himself so he could hide, so he could isolate himself. I also saw that my aunt was in on the secret and that she contributed to the isolation of our house. I understood it so well that I determined not to interfere with their pact.

When I went to bed, my sadness was immense, but at the same time it felt restful to me: it was like reaching dry land; I suffered because of something truly painful, but I was not struggling with myself like other times in those anguished adventures of my imagination. I was still capable of truly suffering for someone; my soul was not entirely lost.

That night I slept marvelously.

It was impossible for me not to tell them at home about the new activities I had come up with for myself. I thought of speaking only with my aunt, but I didn't feel like watching her roll her eyes without letting me finish, and it was hard for me to talk with my father, especially since I had found out about his condition, because I tried too hard to make sure he understood, and my effort blocked his comprehension even more than his own befuddlement.

I decided to speak to them when they were together. So one morning I went out, bought some brushes, and proceeded to clean my father's pipes while he was having coffee. I began to talk about my studies in an offhand way, and I deliberately began by recalling how my aunt had complained about me neglecting my books, which was what had led doña Luisa to arrive at her decision. Given that, my aunt had not much choice but to consent, since she had provided the initiative, but her complaints started up right away, as if what I had been saying meant: Because of what you said, I will never study in my whole life.

Of course the poor thing was not opposed for even a moment. All she did was repeat:

'We'll see what God wills, we'll see what God wills.'

Fortunately, my father cut short her complaints, because it occurred to him to ask how this couple was to be repaid for their efforts on my behalf. I told him that the teacher knew them well, and that she said they were people who never accepted payment; they were doing for me what they had done for other children, from their love of learning and nothing more.

'That's what I don't understand,' my father exclaimed, perplexed, 'that people work for the sake of working!'

I saw immediately that the idea was distasteful to him. My father had a very particular idea of work. When people talked about my Uncle Alberto, who had created such a good position for himself in Bern, he always said: 'My brother is very hardworking,' as if he were saying: 'My brother is completely crazy.'

Right away I tried to get him thinking of an example that would be closer to his own frame of reference.

'I'm surprised you would be the one to say that,' I told him. 'I don't think everything you did in Africa was done because they paid you.'

'Of course not, of course not!' he exclaimed immediately. 'But that's very different. I . . . it's my duty; what do you expect a soldier to do? I don't call that working.'

'Naturally,' I said, 'and they don't call it work when they spend a few hours with their books. The same as you, exactly the same. They do what they do because they care about it, not because of the money.'

'All right, all right,' my father said, 'go ahead. It will be Christmas in a few days and we can give them a nice present.'

I had finished cleaning his pipes and was getting ready to leave. As I said goodbye to my father, he was staring at me.

'You've become such a talker,' he said, 'that you're quite capable of making a man see black as white.'

My only thought was: Why such struggle, such fuss, such juggling over anything that comes up?

On the other hand, I have to admit that neither my father nor my aunt ever found it difficult to spend money on my whims. I ordered the books through the mailman. He brought them right away, along with the bill, which they paid without saying another word.

My lessons began regularly, although not punctually, some days from five to six, others from six to seven, and we began them even though it was already December, so it seemed absurd to think of a vacation when I had spent a year without studying. Besides, my professor said those were exactly the days he did not have to go to the Archive so he could spend more time with me and then I would have no trouble proceeding on my own.

No trouble! My head was like a rusty machine; I spent the mornings studying and I would hold my forehead between my hands as if to support it over the books. It was impossible to keep my imagination from wandering. I reproached myself constantly, because I knew that once I got to doña Luisa's house, even though I set my things up in the study with great seriousness, she would come by every five minutes to offer me one suggestion or another. It was useless; I would be closed up in my room, but my thoughts were in that study; it was as if I continually saw her come in, poke her head through the door, and remind me of the thousand stupidities that never stopped worrying me.

I was tormented continually by the thought that I might have mismeasured for the shelves, or that the heater might not be lit properly, or that it might go out before I arrived.

All these worries obsessed me while I was at home. Later, once I was there, I didn't think about anything, but I could not study either. Then what started up was the fear that the door would suddenly open and those inopportune questions would scare off my concentration, but when doña Luisa did finally appear, speak rather timidly and quickly disappear, I would be left with the worry that I had not been very nice to her, that she might have been able to guess that her things no longer interested me.

It was so difficult to know if she felt hurt, or annoyed, or happy about something that there was no way to employ a tactic with her; the truth was, though, she was saddened and disoriented by the events she herself had precipitated.

The worst thing was, her husband made it abundantly clear to her that the interruptions were inappropriate. He would answer her sharply when she came in to ask something; he glanced furiously at her each time she opened the door, and when she left, he said goodbye with a little smile that seemed to mean: Be patient.

I don't know why, but when I saw that not even one line of her features changed expression, I always thought: She is not serene, serenity is what she lacks; all she has is tenacity.

I watched her wander around the house in circles like someone who has lost something, like the child who has given away his toy and then misses it, like a person who wants to repair something irreparable; but she didn't give up, she was biding her time, and, finally, one day she won.

When I got to her house, I met her in the vestibule; she looked the same as always, but she seemed more direct, livelier.

'Do you know what day this is?' she asked me immediately.

'The twenty-second,' I answered.

'That's right. Tomorrow the doctor is taking us to Valladolid in his carriage, to go shopping.' And she added: 'Do you want to come?'

Before, she would never have asked that. I shrugged my shoulders, without hesitating, as if to say there was no need to ask.

'We have to think carefully about what we need,' she said.

I left my books on the desk in the study and went with her to the dining room. When don Daniel came he started to make a fuss because we had interrupted our routine, but she skirted every possible objection by telling him:

'What do you expect? These next two days are sacred.'

Why recall the same old family argument? It lasted about as

long as usual and ended like all the others. At 7:30 I was ready, waiting on the balcony for the doctor's carriage.

No sooner had I seen it turn the corner than I was running down the stairs; I opened the door, and jumped inside before it could come to a complete stop. The doctor did stop, though, and got down from the driver's seat to give us another blanket that was under the seat inside.

The carriage was comfortable and well enclosed all around, it had magnificent cushions on the seats and on the floor there were lambskins that your feet sank into.

The doctor helped us bundle ourselves up in the blankets. On the one side doña Luisa, the nursemaid, and the baby. On the other, Luisito and I. I put him on my lap so he could warm his legs on mine and we wrapped ourselves up to our chins in the blanket.

Before he closed the door, the doctor spoke to doña Luisa:

'Last night when your husband said he might come with us, I knew very well he'd stay wrapped up in the covers and the rest of us would be the ones to go traipsing out into the early morning frost.'

'So did I,' she answered.

The door closed and the carriage began to move.

Since we were facing each other, we looked at one another without talking, but I could tell, although there was barely enough light to see, that she was speaking to me with her eyes: This is great, isn't it? Just great.

I smiled at her, my face sticking to Luisito's, and he smiled with me.

When it began to get light I began to notice how dressed up she was. I had never seen her in city clothes and I thought she looked wonderful. She was wearing a very heavy, checked, tobacco-colored coat with large otter lapels, and her hat was a small *canotier* of the same color, with a velvet ribbon.

53

Suddenly I remembered what my father had said several days before. I had to come up with a nice present; no doubt I could find something appropriate that afternoon in one of the stores. But what kind of present and for which one of them? Something for the dining room would hardly be special; for the study it would be difficult, because the walls were going to be completely covered with shelves, and something for the desk was unthinkable: that was the monkey's kingdom and even a gift from a sultan would not depose him. Suddenly I had an idea, and it must have lit up my face so much that doña Luisa asked me:

'What are you thinking about?'

'Nothing,' I told her, 'a plot, I was hatching a plot, but I can't tell you for several days.'

She thought I was being evasive and didn't ask anything more. The baby had been sleeping the whole time, totally hidden in large white shawls; picking him up, she said:

'I'm thinking that I better give him something before we get there, because it's the time he usually eats.'

This was difficult, although she managed it somehow. She looked so funny with her *canotier* and her hunter's lapels half open; her left breast peered between them, with one large vein so visible it resembled a *y* drawn with blue ink.

I watched her from my seat and thought: How nice it would be if instead of those ordinary blankets from Palencia her feet were wrapped in one of those felt blankets that look like leopard skin. I have to find one. I said to myself, and I turned to look out through the curtains of the carriage so she would not see me smile again.

We were already in La Rubia; I looked as we passed 'Eden,' the picnic spot I loved in the summer when its grove of trees was thick with blackbirds, and among the bare branches I saw the tables on their little balconies overlooking the river. Everything was covered with a down of frost.

54

Although the sun was high in the sky, it had no warmth. When we arrived near ten, it was dreadfully cold, but the streets teemed with life.

The doctor left his carriage on Miguel Iscar Street, at the house of a druggist where there was an empty lot; we said goodbye to him and agreed to meet there later.

We went immediately to the Val market, and from it to the Campillo market. We left there accompanied by a boy who took everything to the druggist's; he was loaded with celery, thistles, red cabbages, and sea bream.

Afterward, we bought sausages from the pork butchers in the colonnade and olives and little kegs of oysters in the groceries. Finally we reached Rodríguez's.

Because there was such a crowd, it had been necessary to put away the little tables, but they had left one in a corner at the back; it was empty because the people, mostly women, all jammed together at the counter.

We settled the nursemaid in the corner with the children and braced ourselves to struggle with the other women.

'I'm thinking,' doña Luisa said, 'that it's already noon and the baby hasn't had anything for two hours; it would be better to feed him now because who knows when we'll get out of here?'

Of course she repeated this exercise every day, every two hours, but at home it made no difference whatsoever. That day, on the other hand, it turned into an ordeal, and we had the feeling she had to repeat it every five minutes.

She sat down between the small table and the corner, angling the chair a little toward the wall, and settled the baby once more between her lapels.

She positioned herself so discreetly that no one could see what she was doing. Resting her elbow on the small table, she turned her head around and said to me:

'Start working your way up there, and place the order as soon as you get to the counter. You know what we need, just the little marzipan figures, the candied almonds, and the noodles for the almond soup. The nougat we'll get at the Valencians'.'

I tried to accomplish my mission, but there was not a single crack in that crush of women, and I was about to faint from suffocation when I heard a scream: an 'ay!' not very loud but really terrible! I turned and saw that doña Luisa was getting up and handing the baby to a lady next to her. I did not understand what was happening; I only saw that she kept screaming, 'Oh, my God! Oh, my God!' with a voice that got shriller and shriller.

She was holding a handkerchief, digging her nails into it, and tearing at the cloth. Not a single muscle in her face had tightened, but in her eyes there was something like a blindness so intense it seemed certain to end in insanity.

A chorus had formed around the lady holding the baby. I don't know how, but I managed to get next to her and I saw that the baby was purplish and stiff and that he seemed to have stopped breathing. It did not last more than a second; he responded immediately, milk spurted from his little nostrils, and he started to cry; I snatched him away from the woman and carried him to his mother.

'He's fine now,' I shouted, 'it was nothing, absolutely nothing!' But she did not hear me. I tried to put the baby in her arms so she would believe me, but I realized she could not take him: she was still completely on edge, tearing at the handkerchief, and for the first time I saw a straight crease form between her eyebrows. With that crease she shook off her suffering and got hold of herself.

'Ay, what a terrible scare,' she said letting herself sit down, 'what a dreadful scare!'

We got out of that store, through all those women and their comments.

'Let's not be choosy about where we eat,' doña Luisa said. 'We need a bowl of good hot soup right away.'

We went into the Castilla.

By the time we had eaten, everything had passed, and we went back to our shopping. After we bought what we needed, we still had time to walk through the toy stores, buying things for her little boy. He wanted to stop at every one of the stands in the colonnade, and I kept pulling him along.

'Come on,' I said, 'there are better things at Guillén's.'

His mother told me he was too little to know the difference, but I dragged them there, got them inside the store, went from the section with toys to the one with travel items, and there, on a bottom shelf, right within reach, was the blanket just as I had imagined it, exactly the same. All I did was point it out with my eyes, and doña Luisa ran her hand over it.

'How soft it is,' she said. 'It looks like a little wild animal lying there.'

Then I let them go back to the toys.

We were walking toward the carriage when doña Luisa exclaimed:

'The fruit! We forgot to buy some holiday fruit; all we have are pomegranates.'

We walked up the first part of Santiago Street again. There we went into that tiny fruit store where they always have so much fruit from other countries. It seemed incredible that you could breathe such cold air outside and then walk into the smell of pineapples from South America and limes hanging on the walls in great garlands.

At that moment I realized don Daniel had not come. I thought: If he had come, he would have talked about all of this! Of course I can tell him about it, but if I tell him it will just be something silly. On the other hand, if he were to tell me . . . I was seeing it and it seemed like something he had told me.

There were flowers in one corner of the store, some wretched flowers they had left to be thrown away, and on a wooden bench there were pieces of stem and bits of string, as if they had been making bouquets. Among those things I found a very small tea rose. The bud was so tiny it had been overlooked there, hidden in some leaves. I picked it up, thinking to ask the clerk for it, but no one paid any attention to me so I decided to take it. When we went out, I pinned it on doña Luisa's lapel.

'Where did you find one so beautiful?' she exclaimed. 'I was looking at the flowers myself and regretting that none were nice enough to buy.'

We walked along talking about flowers, making plans to plant tulips in the spring and chrysanthemums in the fall. All the way to the druggist's she was explaining to me all the things involved in growing them.

When we got there, the druggist began to put our purchases into the carriage. The doctor followed us back and forth, helping to transfer the packages. In the meantime, I was suggesting to her in a low voice that she ask him if it would be too much trouble to stop for a minute at my grandmother's house so I could run up and say Merry Christmas, because it would not seem right if they found out I had been in Valladolid and not gone to see them.

My request was granted, and ten minutes later I was bursting like a whirlwind into the parlor where my grandmother was doing her knitting and my two aunts were embroidering.

Kisses, exclamations. All three of them spoke at once: 'You're completely changed, you're completely changed.'

I said as much as one can in such a short space of time. I kissed them again and as I was leaving I drew my Aunt Inés into the hall. There I explained that my Aunt Aurelia had asked me to relay carefully all the particulars about something she needed her to do. It was about buying a present she wanted to give.

They were planning to send a note the next day with the mailman, but in order to avoid any misunderstanding I had agreed to explain everything to her precisely. I described the color, size, and location of the blanket in such detail she could have gone to buy it with her eyes closed.

When I got back, we set out again toward Simancas, and we spent another long stretch in the semidarkness of the carriage, not speaking so as not to waken the children.

It had been a good day; there had been that one dreadful moment in the sweetshop, but calm had returned and I felt sure those well-formed features, which resembled the perfect features found only on the figures they use to decorate coins or the borders of diplomas, would remain wrapped in shadows, motionless as always, until we got home.

From where I sat, all I could see was the tea rose, which seemed to be placed perfectly on the otter lapel.

It would be stupid to let myself off the hook: in the next two days I plunged more passionately than ever into just the things I meant to avoid.

Those days, all the cleverness I invested in my daily intrigues, which usually left me feeling very proud inside because I congratulated myself on my loftiness of purpose, I invested unrestrainedly in nothing but trivialities.

I do not remember how I dragged the doctor to my house, even less how I got him to say that it was not right for me to miss out on the joy of those holidays just because my father categorically refused to celebrate them in his home. I do not remember how I hinted that he should offer to be the ambassador of doña Luisa's invitation; the thing is he did agree to explain how, being a bachelor without a family, he would have supper in the home of his friends both evenings, and how it would be no trouble for him to walk me home. After all, that was the real issue.

Christmas Eve night passed quickly, because doña Luisa had promised to play in the choir for the midnight Mass, and everything was prepared quickly and simply so even the maids could attend.

The girls who were going to sing the carols came to practice in the afternoon, so we did not have much time to get ready.

'These days are sacred,' doña Luisa had said, and that phrase went through my head often as a justification for everything. I remember thinking of it many times as I lifted a pot lid. There was a mystery, a magic energy in the smells of those days.

As we opened the oven where the turkey was browning in butter, as we sprinkled cinnamon on the hot almond soup, as we cut stalks of celery over the salad of escarole and pomegranates, the smells of those things spoke to us and kept us in a state of animation that let us rush from one chore to another without getting tired.

Our hands were damp and cold and our cheeks burned as we leaned over the fire, but we worked happily and tirelessly, exchanging a glance each time a whiff of fragrant steam passed by our noses.

'You'll see, you'll see,' doña Luisa told me, fully confident of her skill.

The table wanted for nothing. When doña Luisa had placed the holly wreath, she said:

'This would be prettier with a soft light, but I'm going to use a bright one; a cheery light is better since the four of us flies are all by ourselves'; and she put a large bulb under the shade.

The fact that there were so few of us was exactly the thing I found so wonderful, and it was quite different from the Christmases at my grandmother's where there were always more than twenty people around the table who had nothing to say to each other and who got all worked up over nothing just so they could generate a bit of excitement.

The well-lit table and the bright holly decking the mantel were the only things that gave our celebration a bit of character. Otherwise, we ate all those exquisite things almost in total silence, and there was not even the popping of corks; in don Daniel's hands the champagne bottles lost their corks without making a sound, emitting only a fine gauzelike vapor as they were held over the cups.

Doña Luisa could drink only champagne because she was nursing, so that was all they served during the meal. Afterward, when it was time for dessert, she urged everyone to have something else, and she had brought to the table a small cart on wheels; its two stories were loaded with all kinds of bottles.

Doña Luisa picked up two of them, giving me the mischievous look she had at such times. She poured a glass, which she handed the doctor to pass to me. 'This one goes with the nougat — it's Cariñena,' she told me, 'and then this one with the coffee'; and she also passed me a small glass of Marie Brizard.

Don Daniel pulled the table toward him and began to inspect that battalion. He commented on each of the labels with their lettering and designs from all the countries in Europe, as if they were books. He uncorked the bottles, smelled them, and passed them to the doctor: they sampled everything.

There was also a box of cigars on the little table; I noticed that there were no ashtrays and it occurred to me to go into the study and look for some. When I returned, the doctor had taken my chair. 'You lost your place, but I moved to the head of the line,' he said to me.

Everyone laughed, but to me his joke seemed nasty and common.

Nothing could be done about that now. The two of them had moved toward the corner of the table, and the little table filled with bottles stood between them. They had lit two cigars and were already talking about the same thing as always.

I don't know what it was about, their endless conversation that began every day at the door of the castle; it was special somehow, but not secret; they always talked in loud voices in front of everyone, as though no one could understand even though they heard, which was the truth. I would bet that even of those two, only one understood.

Also, in those two minutes I was gone the nursemaid had appeared in the dining room with Luisito; he would not go to sleep once he realized his mother was missing, and he insisted on being taken to her.

He had not been dressed, but they had wrapped him in a wool shawl. Doña Luisa settled him in her lap and began to give him some of everything that was left on the table: glazed fruit, marzipan . . . I took the chair the doctor had left and moved over to her, at the corner opposite from the talkers.

The arrival of the child had wound up isolating us, and I said to myself desperately: If he hadn't come, maybe we would have moved over there too; but no, we would not have moved over there then either, because doña Luisa did not feel distant.

This was what I could not understand. She knew more about everything than I did. She was truly well informed, but even so she did not suffer from having to remain at that distance, because she never stopped paying a certain attention to what they were saying. She participated two or three times; I don't know if she said anything brilliant or not, but once, when don Daniel hesitated about a book they were discussing, she spoke up immediately: 'That book's in crate three.' Without even turning her head, without letting her attention wander from the two fingers holding a piece of almond nougat on which Luisito chewed quietly.

Why, on the other hand, was I not only unable to say even one word but also incapable of detaching my five senses from there?

A thousand times I was at the point of asking her what they were talking about, but I was afraid her answer would not shed any light for me, even though it would be accurate. I felt that I lacked the beginning, that I would never be able to understand without having heard what they said before, not a few minutes before, but days before, centuries before. Because the truth was the words were the ones they used every day. I heard the word love a few times, but I knew they were not talking about loves.

At last it seemed to me that I understood they were talking about someone, but I didn't know if it was someone they knew or if it was a legendary character. They alluded to what he did or said on a certain occasion. 'When I like him the most,' don Daniel said, and I remember this point by point, 'is when he sets out to consider the vicissitudes of life.' Those were his exact words, and then he added: 'The part about the lizard that traps the fly.' Then he was silent.

'If he would go on and tell about that, I'd understand,' I said to myself. 'It seems to be something quite simple.' But he did not go on; everyone must have known that story about the fly and the lizard.

I looked at doña Luisa and yes, she knew, but even if she had told me the story, she would not have made it possible for me to enter into the conversation.

The doctor was speaking with his opaque voice, in which you could not count on seeing a single bright speck. Suddenly don Daniel interrupted him: 'No, saintliness is not the best thing about Saint Augustine.'

I felt as though someone had hit me on the head: so that's what they were talking about!

A wave of sadness, of terror, of remorse overpowered me like a dreadful threat, as if there had been someone in front of me looking at me mercilessly.

My God, why, why talk about Saint Augustine on that occasion and make me remember his terrible mother?

63

Struggling as if I were trying to break out of a nightmare, I forced myself to open my eyes, telling myself that if that was what they were talking about there was no reason for me not to understand; but I shifted my gaze from one to the other and felt my understanding dragging in it like a fly with wet wings. Something heavy, something sticky was sapping my agility: that meal, those wines weighed on my eyelids as if my face were near a flame.

That much was clear; I could have understood it with less intelligence than I had left at the moment; the rest, never.

The words that reached me grew mysterious again; once again I had no idea about the meaning of the facts or anecdotes they alluded to.

Saint Augustine was probably as far from his mother as that corner of the table was from the one where I sat; the one where we sat, we women. The only thing you could make out from there was not Saint Monica's voice, and she at least was someone, but the voice of her governess and those words of caution: 'When you're a housewife and you hold the keys to the pantry . . .'

But did that really apply to us? Did that have anything to do with doña Luisa, sitting there with her forehead like an angel, with her nose like a small column in the middle of her face, with her little boy asleep on her breast? . . .

This time I was looking at her when I felt my eyes close in order to hide a rush of tenderness full of sadness and confusion.

'Are you sleepy?' she asked me. I nodded. She reached out one of her hands, leaving her arm stretched across the table; I took the hand between the two of mine and felt my head was about to drop onto it, but I resisted for another minute.

At that point the conversation was no more than noise for me. I could not even manage to distinguish one word from the other, but in the gestures and in the features of the two men I could at least understand how things were going.

The doctor's cheeks were flushed and shiny; he was moving his head and hands clumsily, and from time to time he leaned against the back of his chair. Don Daniel was pale, as always, and he remained erect, without letting his body touch the chair. When he was not speaking, he held the cigar with his teeth, tightening his lips with an expression that looked like a smile but was not. Only his eyes sparkled more than usual, but with a dark brilliance. It seemed as though they were more brilliant and more shadowy at the same time.

His hands moved as gracefully as ever. The bottle of kirsch kept emptying into his cup, but he seemed increasingly agile and quick.

Still watching him, I rested my cheek on doña Luisa's hand, which I was still holding, and I stayed that way, stretched out there on the table, for a long time. I don't know if I was asleep or not. At least I had stopped struggling to understand; I closed my eyes and in my head I continued to caress all those beloved things. It was a way of claiming a moment when I could rise above myself.

I left there almost unconscious; all I remember is that the cold made me start to realize I was walking home beside the doctor. The pavement on the streets seemed as strange to me and as close to my face as if I were walking on all fours. That man, who was perhaps no steadier on his feet than I was, was enough to lead me, and if I had happened to fall he would have picked me up; even so, we were not friends, definitely not. At the door, the thanks I gave him were no less frosty than the air, and that's how those two sacred days ended.

I could have spent New Year's Eve there too, but I didn't want to annoy my family any more so I agreed to stay home and go to bed at nine.

I only went to doña Luisa's house in the afternoon. In the morning they had sent the maid to take her the blanket, which had not been delivered until then.

I was full of doubts when I sent it off. The moment when the idea had occurred to me was so far away that I thought it seemed like the most meaningless and inappropriate gift I could have given her. Finally, though, once it was gone, what could I do but make up my mind to face whatever effect it might have produced?

When I arrived, the blanket was on the dining room table, beside the large box it had been delivered in, along with all its wrapping papers and ribbons. Doña Luisa was stroking it just as she had in the store; she loved it.

'What do you think, what do you think of the idea this girl had?' she asked don Daniel when he came in.

Instead of answering her, he stood there looking at me with his hands in his pockets.

'I think that if you were a young man,' he said to me, 'you would have a gift for giving presents to the ladies. I also think that sometimes you would very much like to be a young man.'

What did he mean by that? I don't know. At one moment I thought he understood me, that he realized I was unhappy with how I was, but no, I'm not sure that's what he meant.

I laughed, a little bewildered, but I was thinking that before long he could explain it to me. Soon we would be returning to our long periods of studying and resuming those lessons that no matter how they began always held some oasis, some unexpected island where you could find whatever you wanted.

The year had ended, but nothing changed, no new life began; on the contrary, we seemed to live on the leftovers from the year before; everything was drying up, everything was dying away.

The first two months of this year seem so distant to me! What happened in those sixty days? Nothing: it rained and snowed and we lived our lives, dead as doornails.

Maybe I was the only one who felt stifled like that; the fact is when I remember what I did during those two months, the only way I can protect myself from the shame I feel is by thinking that there must have been some mystery in it all, because I cannot say things defeated me. I had my projects, my desires, my ambitions, and no one opposed me; I myself was the one who languished as if she had fallen asleep.

That's impossible! It's impossible, seeing how I am now, that I could have been like I was a few months ago, and it scares me to think I might experience those gaps all my life, that from time to time I'll fall into those pits.

There is no point in writing this, it's infinitely stupid and embarrassing. Nevertheless, I need to say it; I want it to serve as a reminder to my pride. There is nothing special about me; there are some brief periods when I rise to marvelous heights and then I fall to what I am, the same as anyone else. The fact is, during those months, after trudging through the snow and the mud to get to doña Luisa's house, I would close myself up there in the study, in front of an open book, and not even look at it; but it was not because I was dreaming or thinking of other things. No, I was not thinking about anything; my hands would be blue with cold, and after rubbing them I would pull myself together little by little, and most of the time I would make spit bubbles.

That's the honest truth. I would make a small bubble between my lips and catch it with the tip of the penholder I held in my hand; then I would make another and catch it with the point of my pencil, and finally I would join them together so they made one great big one.

It was very difficult; they almost always burst, but sometimes I would manage to join three or four.

It seems impossible, but that was only several months ago.

By March things were different. During the first days, the weather was still dreadful, but the light had already changed and with the hint of spring a person felt daring enough to defy the cold.

The man who came to work in our garden told me his wife had just had a beautiful baby boy, and I promised to go see it. They lived on a vegetable garden they tended on the other side of the river, and one day after dinner I went to their house. My aunt made up a package of things for his wife.

In their fireplace under the funnel of the chimney there was that very pure smell of burnt broom, and the bit of smoke escaping into the room made the air heavy. The doors and windows were closed so the baby would not catch cold.

Over in the corner where they had the crib, there was a sharper smell so strong it wiped out the others.

The baby was a very fat, bloated little thing squirming in his woolen covers. He seemed content and uncomfortable at the same time, not because anything bothered him but because he was struggling with that uncertainty newborns have. It seemed to me that the strong smell smelled of his bad mood.

I stayed there a long time; they stuffed me with sweets. Finally I left and when I went out it felt like the cold was digging its nails into my eyelids and my nose.

I had already started to cross the bridge, on my way back toward town, when I saw a girl coming toward me who looked like a servant in one of the better houses. She had a basket over her arm and I thought she was probably taking a present to the gardener's wife.

I noticed her right away, but I did not realize that she was walking slower and slower and that automatically I slowed down as well. I don't know why but I never suspected for a minute that she would stop, but when I got close to her I stopped; I peered over the railing and she peered over too. I was looking at the water, but out of the corner of my eye I saw that the girl kept putting her hand into the basket and throwing something into the river. One, two, three, four little things fell to the water before I realized: they were four puppies. I turned then and saw the horrible face on that girl. Of course I had always known people throw puppies into the river when they don't want to raise them, but I never thought a young girl could do it!

We were almost at one end of the bridge. The water was not deep there and it lingered among the stones and roots along the river bank, swirling around them. The puppies remained there for a long time, struggling in one of those pools; it seems impossible, but they swam, managing to float, flailing their arms the way newborns do, with a desperation so intense even the freezing water could not manage to kill it.

Finally the current carried them away.

From up there I went over the ways I could go down and pull them out, but it was very difficult; when I got to them it would already have been too late, because they probably could not have survived after that dunking.

By the time they went off in the current they were like little old people.

I thought I saw the girl about to make some comment and I ran off so as not to meet her eyes again.

I no longer felt the cold; my body was much colder than the air. It seemed impossible that I would ever get to doña Luisa's. I had to concentrate all my attention on breathing, and each breath I took seemed to me to be my last. The shock I had just experienced had been erased from my imagination; all I could think about now was the need to take a breath, and another, and still another.

I got to the front door and walked through the hallway without realizing I had gone in, without noticing that the temperature in the house was different from the one outside.

When I went into the dining room they looked at me with alarm. I don't know how, but I explained what I had seen, and doña Luisa exclaimed:

'You've had a real shock; take a drink of water.'

Don Daniel grabbed the glass of water from her.

'What a suggestion,' he shouted, 'a glass of water! Don't you see she's been completely traumatized?'

He poured a couple inches of rum into the glass and made me drink it in one swallow. He led me to the study; on the sofa there were several pillows and the felt blanket; it looked as though he had taken his siesta there.

He made me lie down on the sofa, wrapped me in the blanket, and said: 'Sleep for a while.'

He went toward the door, and as he left he turned to look at me; he stood there for a long while, leaning on the door frame and looking at me.

Although a lot of time has gone by, I still do not understand; it will take years for me to understand his gaze, and sometimes I hope I will have a long life so I can look at it for as long as I live; sometimes I think that no matter how much I look at it there is no point in understanding it now.

A smile began to appear around that gaze, or rather something like a smile that made me smile. It was as if he could see, inside my eyes, the horror I had seen. He too seemed to be looking at something monstrous, something that caused him an unspeakable terror, but he was smiling just the same.

I felt the rum begin to wrap me in a rush of warmth; I stopped looking at him, and I don't know how long he stood in the doorway. I fell asleep breathing deeply: I was still thinking about taking breaths.

When I opened my eyes, I saw there was a bit of sun shining in the garden. The sky had been overcast all day, but as the sun set it peered through some wisps of what seemed to be the last clouds, and they were the last clouds of winter.

The next day, when I got there, it seemed as though no one was home. I saw the cook at the far end of the garden.

'Isn't doña Luisa here?' I shouted to her.

'Yes,' she said, 'she's on the sun porch.'

I found her beneath that raw light, since there were still no leaves on the arbor. She was holding a mirror and a pair of tweezers, searching out some half-dozen gray hairs you could see on her temples.

'Listen,' she said as soon as she saw me, 'don't call me doña Luisa anymore. I'm really not so old.'

'Not so old nor old at all,' I told her. 'You seem ageless, as if you were born just like you are now.'

She preferred not to notice the compliment in my words.

'I could easily be your mother,' she told me with her usual passivity.

'Well, sometimes,' I answered, 'inside it seems to me that I could be yours.'

'In that case, I'm going to have to respect you,' she replied in the same tone as before.

'Don't say that awful word. I swear the word sounds evil to me. I don't know if it's because it's not necessary when I love someone or if it's because I've heard it used by people I can't love.'

Her face was still unchanged, but her hands shook. What changed them was not a tremor but her uneasiness; several times the mirror and the tweezers passed from one to the other. Was she afraid to keep on with that conversation? Was she not strong enough? Automatically, she gazed into the mirror for a while as if to comfort herself with the serenity of her own image; then she acted as if she heard something.

71

'Don't you think that's Luisito crying?' she asked.

She began to run upstairs; I knew very well the child was not crying.

During those days I started to slip back once again, but not toward stupefaction, the way I did in the winter; further back: I went back to the fantasies and daydreams from when I was very little.

All those absurd games I invented to amuse my imagination when I was not yet serious enough to be concerned with real things came back to send me constantly spinning up in the air. I studied poorly, and I even listened poorly to don Daniel.

I acted as if I were listening to him with rapt attention, but in fact all I did was look at him. I amused myself by watching how the hair grew on his temples, how it was cut around his ears, and how his beard separated into different currents that all started out together from his mouth.

Only on certain attempts was I able to watch him so carefully. While he spoke, I would be thinking about the details I needed; then I would stare at him, as if to understand what he was saying, but it would be to make sure about the way his eyelashes sprouted from the edge of his eyelids all black and shiny, as if they were lacquered.

I would lower my eyes toward the desk, and when he started to speak again I would look at him, studying the outline of his almost straight nose, the shape of his rather pale, rather thin lips. Because they were outlined so precisely, with the curves of one conforming so exactly to those of the other, it seemed that he thought with those lips or that his mouth had been thought, traced: it was a model, what they call a paradigm.

But my madness did not stop at observation. One of the first warm afternoons, when he came in after walking along the road in the sun the whole way from the castle, he tossed his jacket over an armchair and sat down beside the desk. The same as he always did, with his back to the glass door. Soon I began to notice the light passing through his shirt. As he bent over, to lean on the arm of his chair, the way the shirt hollowed a little made it possible to see the lateral part of his torso, not his chest but his side, where his ribs stood out a little, beneath a skin that looked golden amid the whiteness of his shirt.

Just like years before, just like when my imagination used to play those games where no holds were barred and I would let myself go totally, just like that I threw myself into my fantasy, into being alive in that sphere, amid the light of a region that sometimes I saw as a cavern, and other times a jungle. It was a transparent zone I walked in: I commanded it from one end to the other, and I could guess what dawn and dusk would be like there, what each of the seasons would be like.

I have seldom managed to transfer myself so completely to one of those places in my daydreams. I lost myself in it so deeply that don Daniel noticed my absence.

'I don't know what's wrong with you today, but you don't understand anything,' he said. 'Sometimes I'm afraid I make you study too much.'

I protested and gave him a thousand reasons why I was distracted, inventing some petty quarrel at home.

'Whatever the reason,' don Daniel said to me, 'today there's no point in your trying to do anything.'

He closed the book he was holding and stared at me, but not intensely, as if he knew that looking at me would do no good. His gaze fell on me, but it was dull.

I saw in him a confusion and an uneasiness that he did not want to leave unresolved. He knew it was impossible for him to fathom my thoughts, but he at least wanted to pull me out of them.

He opened a drawer in the desk and took out a wooden box, throwing it onto the sofa.

'Here,' he told me. 'Amuse yourself looking at these photographs. In the meantime I'll write a letter.'

I buried myself in the photographs: I wanted to be obedient.

Almost all of them were family portraits and I did not want to interrupt him by asking about each of the people. There were also some pictures of houses and farms in Seville, and I imagined he must have lived in one of those places when he was a child. I set the pictures aside so I could ask about them when he finished writing.

A few minutes later he turned his head; I asked him, and in one of the fields he pointed out the country home that belonged to his parents.

There were other photographs of picturesque spots, with windows covered with grilles and girls peering out between the flowers and boys below with guitars. Don Daniel told me that those kinds of things were staged for tourists, that you no longer see any of them because young people today don't find them entertaining.

'That's too bad,' I said, 'because I like them so much. I don't mean as entertainment, but, well, they're things that to me are precisely . . .'

I didn't finish the sentence, moving my head as if to say my personal preference made no difference.

Don Daniel dropped his pen, came over to the sofa, and sat down as quickly and smoothly as a cat, tucking one leg under him. He began to ply me with questions: why had I spoken so vehemently, he wanted to know. He had seen something flicker on my face that made me respond with such enthusiasm — an event, a memory . . .

I could not refuse; the story was completely stupid, but I told it to him.

He asked so eagerly and with such interest that I set out to tell him the story down to its most trivial details, maybe because

I felt guilty for having so many things in my head I could not tell him.

Since he had never lived in Valladolid, I started by describing my neighborhood for him, and my house on the street that used to be named Cárcava because of the gully, and the stories about all the neighbors that would always be going around there.

There was an early memory that went back to when I was five years old. To be precise, I was probably between five and six when I went to the grocery store with the housekeeper one day and saw two things that were engraved on my mind: some balls of salt they give goats to lick, I don't know what for, and a boy who was sitting there very elegantly without being given any errands and with a very wide-brimmed hat on his head.

A long time afterward I heard about the trouble the storekeeper's son had caused his father, because of his studies, and finally one day the story was that his father had thrown him out of the house. Next came the news that he had gone and become an organ grinder, that they called him 'the Drugster' since he had been in pharmacy school before he dropped out, and that he would beat on his chest until he spit blood, to show people how brave he was.

Then the most important piece of news arrived: he even had the nerve to come and play in our neighborhood.

I would not have recognized him, but I got the servant girl to point him out to me. He had changed a lot and grown extremely thin; he wore a cap with a visor and a kerchief around his neck.

He would usually come around noon and he played a fabulous habanera. I wanted to learn it, and one day I decided to go out on the balcony so I could really hear him; what struck me was how much he looked like the king.

After he played the habanera he began to play some more ordinary things, and then I threw him a few coins, and when he raised his head to thank me I asked if he wouldn't play it again.

This is what I could not really tell about then: the movement he made with his shoulders and eyebrows, as if he were saying I should not doubt it for an instant. 'Whatever you want, baby,' he told me, and he played the habanera three or four times.

'Well, that had almost nothing to do with the photographs after all,' I said, seeing that don Daniel said nothing; and in order to explain why I had told him the story, I stressed that it had been the way he offered, the knowledge that he was playing for me, that I could ask him for whatever I wanted.

While I finished the story, I had been putting the photographs back into the box. Don Daniel kept his eyes fixed on a corner of the study, but he was looking further than the wall would let him: the way he was looking it was as if the scene I had just described hovered in the air like a mirage and he were still studying it.

I could not think that he had stopped paying attention to me, because I knew he was looking at me, but at me on the balcony. Afterward, he started to smile and he smiled at me in the study, like the other time when he only smiled with his mouth.

'Well,' I decided to say, 'I have to leave since it's almost dark; I better get going.'

He leapt up from the sofa with another catlike motion and took hold of my head with both hands, sinking his fingers into my hair; then he grabbed the scruff of my neck as if he were about to drown me. His smile struggled to become a laugh, but he could not manage to laugh. He led me to the door almost in the air and pushed me into the hall.

'Get out of here,' he said. 'Get out of here, you traitor.'

My story had been more successful than I expected, but the success offered me no consolation for the remorse I felt over what had just happened.

At the base of my good behavior there had always been a fear that I might get caught in the act of doing something wrong. I

76

was well aware of this, and I told myself many times that if I did not lie or do worse things it was because I would die from a fit of rage if anyone ever found out I was not perfect. This time, however, I suffered indescribably from the fact that my thoughts would stay walled up and go unpunished; I felt real heartache, without any embarrassment or the least hint of self-love.

And it was not like other times when I longed to be caught doing certain things because I thought they were so impressive.

I don't know why I had never spoken to don Daniel about my crazy thoughts from before. If I had told him about those things, he would have known what I'm capable of and he would have been on to me. Also, I could easily have told him if my backsliding into the same foolishness had not involved him, but the very thing that happened was itself rather secret, and secrets were so against my will I felt as though I had been conquered by some revolting enemy. That term is exactly the one I used to describe the word 'respect.' The ingredient is so murky and so disagreeable if it mixes around things you love! And what's most degrading is how it controls a person even though it only has power on the outside, only where things are visible; inside, what can it do?

When the secret is in its world and knows it will not have to leave those secret places for any reason, nothing can hold it back. I never suffered from scruples like that when I thought I was living inside the Holy Sepulcher, and that was obviously a secret, but only for people outside of it. On the other hand, this new secret weighed on my chest; it kept me awake, confusing me and causing me to think things like: 'It's something I have no right to.' Then, 'Another odious word'! those thoughts would make me exclaim, and I spent the whole night that way.

Daylight was starting to come through the cracks in my shutters and all the noises of the country were starting up; everything was stirring after a rest, but I could not find any way of resting.

Finally I heard the bells from the church of the Arrabal and suddenly it occurred to me: I don't have to go to confession until next month. That idea made me see everything in a different way; time would pass, I thought, and I would feel less agitated and would be able to express my feelings more sensibly. With that certainty I managed to fall asleep, and it was already after eight when I was awakened by an unusual event: a horn honking insistently outside the front door. No one in Simancas had a car.

Unfamiliar voices rushed through the house and one of them belonged to my aunt, who sounded so different I could not tell if she was laughing or crying.

Suddenly I understood: a surprise visit from my Uncle Alberto, his wife, and daughter.

Naturally, for the three days they were with us I did nothing but spend time with them.

My Aunt Frida was okay; above all, she had wonderful clothes. I liked Adriana much more, though: she was the most beautiful girl I had ever seen. She was only a few months older than I was, and she was a little taller and heavier, but she was so childlike you wanted to pick her up in your arms.

We spent the morning in the garden; since Adriana spoke Spanish well, we could talk about all sorts of things. Later, at the table, I learned about their plans for the trip.

My uncle expected to say in Valladolid for several months. He wanted to get some money, which I know nothing about, for his companies in Bern, and he had come with the intention of settling a lawsuit with some other relatives that he and my father had been involved in for a long time.

Of course I was not the least bit interested in that topic, but even if someone had been interested the matter would not have been discussed, because my father refused to hear anything about it: 'Don't consult with me about it at all; do whatever you want, anything you want,' and no one could get him to change his mind.

Since that's how things were, they talked about what my aunt would do. She had no idea of staying in Valladolid. She had already visited the museum and the churches and her plan was to go off in the car with her daughter, touring Spain until September, when she would return to Bern with her husband, or without him if he had not concluded his business.

'Let me take Leticia with us,' Aunt Frida said to my father suddenly. 'She'll have a wonderful time.'

'Don't even talk about it,' my father answered, clenching his teeth.

Adriana jumped from her chair and went over to hug him; she started kissing him on both sides of his face.

'Let her come, Uncle, let her come,' she said.

My father kissed her back, but he kept shaking his head.

'Wait,' I told her under my breath. 'We'll see.'

Aunt Aurelia was feeling almost dizzy. Aunt Frida saw right away that it was a lost cause and began to say that she wanted to see the Archive. The word filled me with dread. They convinced her to wait until the following day, and the whole time they talked I felt as if I were enveloped in the haze of all my past and future guilts. Because suddenly something like the memory of an unanswered question popped into my head, as if the day before everything had been left half finished, although at the same time what was going on right then in my house interested me too much to let myself sink into that memory; so I realized that I was going to stop worrying about it and this tormented me. All I could think of to say was: Why couldn't they have come at a different time, on another day when my relations with the other house were better?

But what happened there? I asked myself afterward. And the truth was that nothing had happened.

Even so, I was aware that my thoughts were running along a worn-out thread when they went in that direction. I could not quite put my finger on the weak point, but I felt it, and in the meantime I listened with my right ear to the incredible things Adriana was telling me.

How funny her accent sounded to me! Between courses, I amused myself by undoing her braids, just for the pleasure of doing them up again.

We cut off their conversation soon after dinner was over, but I don't know how; since I was wrapped up in the flow of my unmentionable worries at the same time I was listening to Adriana, I no doubt alluded to a kind of chore or habit I could not skip, and to the need for her somehow to do it with me that afternoon.

The fact is we walked around the town a few times, talking constantly, and we wound up seated in doña Luisa's dining room when it was time for the children's late afternoon snack.

I cannot remember what I said when we went in; everything must have been perfectly natural, but I have the impression that I was deaf for a long time.

I must have said something, but neither my words nor the words of anyone else produced sound in my ears. All I remember, as if I had watched it through a hole, is doña Luisa turning the Russian coffeepot, which was in the middle of the table with the flame in its burner flickering, and Adriana, Luisito, and me watching her silently.

We all had cups of hot milk in front of us. Doña Luisa went from one to the other, adding a stream of hot coffee and lumps of sugar to each cup; then we ate coffee cakes and all kinds of rolls. Then, another space.

After that, without being able to remember how he came in, or what I said to explain why I was not studying, I saw don Daniel serve himself a cup of coffee, drink it standing up, in one gulp, and go out the door. I know he spoke with me and Adriana, though, because otherwise she would not have told me that she thought he seemed very nice. The only thing I remember is something he said to doña Luisa as he walked behind me on his way out. It was something like: 'You are seeing now that this young rose has completely turned into a rambler on me.'

From the haze of that afternoon I can still remember another conflict, which has floated above everything else for me: although she had asked me several days before, I had still not decided to call doña Luisa 'Luisa.' But I did not want her to think I'd forgotten she didn't like it, even though I had not accepted the change right away, without her having to insist. That day, especially, in front of Adriana, it would have seemed as though I wanted to show off.

So everything I said was a little forced, as if it were likely to disappear right away.

Finally I started to talk about how we had to make up a bed for Adriana in my room, because her parents would be using the guest room, and that's how it ended.

When we got home, the bed was already made up.

At dinner time, Aunt Frida unpacked a lot of things she had brought for me in her suitcase: a vest with little flowers of different colors embroidered in wool; a pair of very thick socks; some small aprons made of printed batiste.

'These things,' Aunt Aurelia kept asking her, 'are they things little girls wear in your country?'

She hardly answered because she hardly understood the question. I quickly assured her that I thought everything was beautiful, and in truth it was: it was like a landscape.

While her mother was showing us those things, some of which she had made herself, Adriana gave me a package. 'I bought this for you when we left,' she said. 'It's the emblem of the city where I was born.' It was a small bear carved in dark wood; its mouth was open and it had tiny white teeth and a very red tongue.

All I could say was an admiring 'Oh!'

Adriana understood that I liked it. She's a good girl, Aunt Frida stood thinking; how can they know so much? I wondered as I looked at them.

No, I said, it's impossible. I looked at those two pairs of blue eyes and repeated to myself inside that Aunt Frida and Adriana did not know what they had brought with them. Aunt Frida had embroidered those little colored flowers and Adriana had chosen a small bear in the station, but who had given them the pattern for the composite image it all formed? Did they realize that I knew the whole story, or was I perhaps the only one who knew it and they did not?

All I could think about was getting supper over quickly so I could have the whole night to talk with Adriana and ask her things about her country.

As always, reality turned out to be different than I expected, but no less splendid. The stories Adriana told me were not about bears and valleys filled with flowers; they were about her school.

She described their end-of-the-year festivities, where she had played a leading role because she was one of the girls who knew most about things beyond what they studied in school. Her mother had engaged special teachers who went to their house so Adriana would be educated in the arts. She knew how to dance on her toes, and, to show me, she thrust one leg from under the sheets and held her right foot out so it formed a straight line from the tip of her big toe to her thigh. Then she told me that she would dance so I could watch her, if I knew how to hum some of the things she danced to.

'Don't you know anything by Mozart?' she asked me.

'No,' I said.

'How can you not know even one *minuetto?*'

'I've never heard one.'

'Then what do you know?'

'What they play around here.'

'I don't think I'd know how to dance to those things,' Adriana said, and she lay there thinking.

I could tell she was looking for something simple, since she realized how few things I knew.

'I'll dance the pavane for you,' she said suddenly, 'everyone liked it the most. But I need the other girl who danced the marquis. Maybe I can dance both parts myself . . .'

She changed from her nightgown into some little bloomers, stuffed the toes of her shoes with two handkerchiefs she had wadded into balls, put on her socks, and said:

'All set; you'll see: the woman comes out first.'

She hid a little distance behind the wardrobe and came out from behind it unexpectedly.

Of course when she came out she was not wearing anything different than when she hid, but even so she was completely transformed.

With a few indescribable steps, she moved toward the center of the bedroom. She almost never let her heel touch the floor, and when she did it was only to highlight the movements her ankle would make as it raised her entire body, allowing it to balance on the tip of her toe.

The whole time she was humming a very subtle melody, using her hands to hold up her skirt, or she would forget about her hands hanging there from her arms and let her arms sway with the music, first to one side, then to the other, as if they were moved by the wind.

Then, bending one of her knees and stretching the opposite leg out behind her, she began to pick flowers from the floor.

Suddenly she jumped up and disappeared behind the wardrobe, saying:

83

'Now the marquis.'

When she came out, she was a young gentleman balancing a monocle on his nose and quivering a little as he walked. He approached the spot where the lady was gathering flowers and asked her for one; she refused to give it to him. He pursued her, pleading with her and kneeling, while she walked ahead of him indifferently.

She walked ahead of him, because suddenly Adriana made that wonderful movement and wound up on the tip of her toe; then she turned as if her arms were loaded with flowers, gesturing disdainfully around the place where the marquis was kneeling. He held out his hands and then made a few motions as if he were promising her necklaces and earrings. She threw him the flowers and gave him a kiss.

When she gave him the kiss she was totally a butterfly. On the tip of her right foot, her left leg stretched out behind, in the air, almost horizontal; her left arm in the same direction; her body curved slightly toward the man on his knees and her right hand open, holding her chin with the palm, as if she were blowing the kiss.

Then they joined hands and danced the pavane.

Both of them danced because one replaced the other so swiftly that the image of the first was never erased before the second became visible.

Suddenly we heard someone knocking on the wall and Aunt Frida's voice shouting: 'Adrgiana!' We stopped talking. Adriana jumped into bed and pulled the covers up over her head. For the first time I noticed that my aunt said 'Adrgiana.'

'Adriana,' I whispered, 'why didn't they give you a name from your own country?'

She stuck out her head and the expression that came over her face suggested a person about to tell a delightful tale from so long before it can only be remembered with great difficulty.

'You know why?' she said. 'My parents met on the Adriatic. Mama was in Italy studying archaeology . . .'

I did not want to ask her anymore, and I even stopped her by making a gesture to let her know I had understood. Besides, I could tell she was sleepy and I got ready to turn out the light. I remember how just as I did that, at the instant I turned the little knob on the switch, I thought of my father, reproaching myself for not having gone to his room to see that he was settled comfortably in bed and to get him anything he might need, as if that were something I did every night, although I had never done it.

The next day an effort was made to accommodate both the whims of some and the obligations of others, which meant we wound up with a mishmash of crazy things strung together by chance.

From the minute she got out of bed, Aunt Frida began talking about the Archive. What I wanted at any cost was to have Adriana dance for doña Luisa. There was nothing my father wanted. Aunt Aurelia said she saw no choice but to participate. My Uncle Alberto wanted everything everyone else wanted; Adriana, whatever I wanted.

We were all anxious to put our own plans into effect. I got mine ready as fast as I could.

'Before we go to the Archive,' I said, 'Adriana and I will go by doña Luisa's house to see if she has the music for the pieces Adriana dances to and to tell her that we'll spend a while with her late in the afternoon.'

No one objected.

The silence of siesta let us slip out stealthily, as if it were very early in the morning. Once outside, it was better not to run because our street was so steep; we walked on the shady side, close to the wall.

We had not gone more than a few yards when we heard

energetic footsteps gaining on us. Adriana turned around immediately: it was her mother.

'I want to see the town,' she started to say before she caught up to us. 'Why stay at home all the time, always at home? It's crazy!'

We smiled grudgingly.

'Where are you going?' my aunt asked.

'To that house,' I answered, pointing it out.

'Well, I'll leave you at the door and walk around a bit until it's time to visit the Archive. We'll all meet there,' she added. 'I've left them so Aurelia can take her time getting ready, as much time as she likes, and so she can talk to her brother alone for a while. Who knows, maybe she has some little secret to tell him.'

By then we were at doña Luisa's door; Aunt Frida had each of us by a shoulder and she was still making witty remarks about my family. The door was ajar, and inside, a figure walked quickly through the zone of green light. Out of the corner of my eye I saw her take shape as she went about her chores with movements that were always decisive but never hurried. I saw her stop, unavoidably, look down the hallway, and come toward the door; she had heard my voice.

She opened the door all the way, greeted us with her imperceptible smile, and said to Adriana:

'Is this your mother?'

My aunt rushed forward to greet her.

'Won't you come in for a while?' doña Luisa suggested.

The movement she made with her hand, motioning us across the doorstep, seconded her invitation.

There was nothing to do but resign myself: I decided to fall deaf once again.

I liked taking Adriana there so doña Luisa could see her, but it irritated me that Aunt Frida would see everything in the house, everything doña Luisa had done, even though I knew that she would find all of it more than acceptable and that she was well qualified to judge.

We're wasting time, I repeated to myself. Aunt Frida had come to see the Archive, she wanted to see the town, later she would see all of Spain. What put it into her head that she had to see doña Luisa's house as well?

They went into the parlor; I kept Adriana at the door and asked permission to go upstairs to the drawing room.

We ran upstairs, and as I opened the door I said to her: 'Their decorating is still only half finished.'

Adriana paid no attention to me and she ignored the empty drawing room. This was something I appreciated in her. She went to look at the music immediately and set aside a few sheets, saying that she had found her favorite pieces. She opened the piano and played a scale, but I did not let her continue because I guessed the children were still napping.

When we went downstairs we found my aunt alone in the parlor; she had convinced doña Luisa to come with us to the Archive and had made her go and get dressed.

I tugged at Adriana's hand again and took her out to the garden, where I showed her the still empty dovecote, the arbor, the well: it was a day for seeing things.

Finally we left with the two women and saw steep streets from which you could make out the Pisuerga River. We saw the church from all sides and the thick walls of some manor houses; then we went to see the Archive.

Aunt Aurelia and Uncle Alberto were waiting for us at the door. Our visit had been announced to don Daniel, and we all went in as far as his office.

We were only there for a minute, but I saw what it was like where he worked every day, with his desk, his secretaries, and staff.

The whole troop of us, one after the other, paraded through rooms filled with shelves, display cases, and lecterns.

I wanted Adriana to go with me into the deep recesses that opened in the walls around the windows and for us to let the others go on looking at things, because that's where there were really things to see. From some of the openings you could see deep, gray patios; from others, the plain. Everything was there. In some places pieces of broken iron jutted out from the wall and it was impossible to tell what they might have been used for; they seemed to be traces of something that had left its mark in the stone repeatedly.

I was sure that if they would give me a chance to concentrate and sit still for a while on one of the small benches placed sideways in the window openings, I could understand everything, see everything exactly as it had been at another time. But we were not left in peace for even a minute. We had to keep going, to move from one room to another, where there were letters from saints and kings.

'Come here, Adriana; look at this,' my aunt called constantly. She made her take note of a date or some other detail, speaking a few words in Swiss-German to pound it into her head.

After that we saw the cellars, the moats, the doors. Then we went out, at last, into the fresh air; the stars were already shining.

I saw that we had very little time left, but as I prepared to lay claim to it, I realized from the conversation that Aunt Aurelia had invited them to our house and that everyone was walking in that direction.

Unbelievably, the moment of duty had arrived. Aunt Aurelia had to repay them; she repeated this several times a week, and she was taking advantage of that evening when she felt stronger because her brothers could offer their support.

There were sweets and small cups of Malaga. The housekeeper brought the trays and my aunt filled the small cups carefully, as if she were pouring medicine.

I only followed what went on in one corner of the living room. My father had settled himself in his armchair, assuming his role as convalescent once again. Of course this was to be expected since his disability was permanent, but the fact that my uncle had not been in Spain when he returned gave my father a pretext for bringing out the battle stories he no longer told at home, and the dog listened to them attentively. This did not last long, though: Aunt Frida pulled up a chair and went to settle herself beside don Daniel, trying to monopolize his attention with questions about things she had seen in the Archive. He did not want to miss my father's story, which seemed to affect him a great deal, but Uncle Albert could not realize that don Daniel was more interested in what my father was saying than in my aunt's chatter, and he redoubled his attentions to my father, as if he had to shoulder the weight of that painful duty all by himself.

Since they were still separated from the others, Aunt Aurelia took them some more sweets. I seized the opportunity, grabbed doña Luisa by one hand and Adriana by the other and took them to the dining room. I closed the door and started to plead with Adriana to dance:

'It doesn't matter, just like you did it last night. You improvised then, and it was wonderful.'

She resisted, but I would not give up:

'Please dance. If you take a long time to make up your mind, someone will come and then it will be too late. Don't you see that you're leaving tomorrow? If you don't do it now, there won't be another chance.'

Adriana took off her shoes, hid behind the sideboard, and said: 'The lady.'

Her voice was different from the day before, but she started to dance. I was sure she would warm up eventually, but before she could take ten steps the housekeeper burst into the room, walked right in front of her, took a bunch of things from the sideboard, and then marched out.

My eyes traveled from Adriana to doña Luisa's face; I wanted to see if she was as delighted by Adriana as I had been the night before, and I could see that she did like her but that her attention was divided between the dance and my determination to make her appreciate it.

'I've spent the whole day thinking about you having the chance to see it,' I said squeezing her arm. 'It's great, isn't it?'

I could not hear her answer: my aunt appeared, wanting to save doña Luisa from the annoyance she had let herself in for rather than hurt our feelings.

'Come in here, for heaven's sake. These girls have you closeted while they force you to watch their antics.'

Adriana was doing the marquis when my aunt interrupted.

Doña Luisa tried to protest, but there was no use; they made us go into the other room and it was all over.

In the living room everyone kept talking about stupid things. Finally they got up to go home.

When they were at the door, doña Luisa told Adriana again that she had liked her dancing very much. She kissed her twice and said to her what she had said to me the first day:

'Goodbye, dear.'

Then it was my turn, and to me all she said was goodbye. She put her arm around my shoulders, gave me a big hug, and kissed me. She put the kiss on my cheek, next to my eye. I felt her lips between my eyelashes; for a long time she held me against her. The street was dark, and I studied it in her hug, the way blind people read with their fingers. The strength of her thin arm was stamped on my shoulders; against my jaw I felt the bone you could see at the base of her neck, but at the same time she seemed very fragile to me. I don't know if it was the perfume she was wearing or if feeling the mound of her breast made me remember that day I saw her in the carriage, with her transparent skin covered with blue veins.

The hug, the unusually long kiss, helped me to know her better, even though I could still not express what I knew about her. I thought about it the whole night and I thought that such immense tenderness was something I did not deserve.

The visitors left early the next day.

Adriana and I had studied thoroughly the possibilities of my joining them on their trip, and we had come to the conclusion that there were no possibilities; my uncle was the only one who could have managed to come out ahead in those negotiations, and for the moment he needed all the cleverness he could muster to drag a few simple words about their affairs out of my father. We thought that perhaps if they were successful in their lawsuit, Adriana would ask her father if he would celebrate by intervening in our case and maybe winning that victory as well.

Of course I could have won it too, but what that would really have meant was beating my father, and I did not want him to see me side with my uncle.

Ever since my uncle had arrived, it had been clear to me that my father thought he led a charmed life. My uncle was a year older than my father, but he seemed like his son. He wore those light-colored foreign suits confidently; this was amazing because he looked more Spanish than my father, and you could tell he took advantage of that look in Switzerland. My father's blond moustache was already almost white, and he resembled one of those defeated Frenchmen you see in illustrations.

The fact is they left and things went back to the way they were before. Although not entirely the way they were before: Adriana's tracks were not erased from Simancas for a long time.

There was one thing that hurt and disheartened me: people dismissed my fascination with her as childishness.

Only doña Luisa had understood. That was a mystery! I am sure that if I had explained what Adriana meant to me, it would not have been doña Luisa who understood the best; nevertheless, she had only needed to look at my face a few times as I squeezed her arm in the dining room.

On the other hand, don Daniel had said to me the next day: 'What, so the little marzipan girl is gone?'

And he had started to come late to class.

Even in his explanations there was suddenly a coldness, as if he were sorry that he had taken me so seriously before.

What could I do? Make a speech that would tell him what I thought about Adriana? I felt totally incapable of that. If I had not been able to infect him with my emotion, how was I going to convince him with reasons that would probably sound totally awkward?

I was withdrawing too; instead of studying I would make doña Luisa sit down at the piano and play for me only the pieces that Adriana had set aside. She did not hesitate to oblige me.

The girls from the choir had stopped coming some time before; her children would keep each other entertained on the sun porch off the dining room, and we would settle ourselves in the drawing room, which filled with music the way a glass fills under a stream of water.

The drawing room was still empty, but it no longer had that look of an attic with rolled-up cables over the door and matchboxes on the floor: it was clean now, the windows spotless, the shutters scrubbed with potash and the dais with sand. Doña Luisa never had time to go to the auctions in Valladolid and look for the antique furniture she wanted.

To listen to her I chose the farthest of the balcony openings. I would sit on the floor, lean my back against the shutter, and watch all the shapes sketched by that music like patterns for Adriana's dancing. Everything was marked there: her small steps, her bows and curtsies. The light would fade but doña Luisa would keep playing because she played from memory.

Sometimes Adriana's image disappeared; although the music always resembled her music, it took on a more dramatic cast. I would call it more heroic. The tempo no longer followed the gestures of gathering flowers or greeting a lady. There was something desperate in it, even though that did not keep it from being serene. I sensed an attempt to express danger, something like being at the edge of death. The motions expressed by those shapes were no longer from dance, but from fencing.

Marvelous ghosts passed through the semidarkness of the drawing room, but sometimes I could not help watching the only real form there, with her wide bony shoulders, her thin voile dress, and her red mules sliding on the pedals.

In spite of those shoulders, as she played I saw her fragility once again. The chestnut curls were never fastened on her head, but when they were tossed to the music they got even more disheveled, and I wondered if it might not be harmful for her.

This has happened to me several times before: at moments of great emotion, when my five senses seem to be absorbed in something, I have suddenly seen, off to the side like that, something else completely removed from whatever caused my emotion, as if my faculties increased tremendously and overflowed the region where they seemed to be confined. These visions are not enough to distract my attention, but they are not forgotten either: they keep hovering around my principal emotions like satellites, without ever evaporating.

Below, in the study, the doctor had even appeared again. When I would go down from the drawing room and hear that the famous conversation was already under way, I would feel myself drowning as if I were shipwrecked in my own anger. 'Why do I come?' I would say to myself. 'How could I have ever believed sometimes that I would eventually count for something here?' But I would go in and open a book, or say I had already studied at home.

93

Don Daniel would come toward the desk and speak to me condescendingly. Meanwhile, the doctor's arm would reach over my head and draw a cigar from the monkey; then he would go to a corner of the study, murmuring a few words with the cigar protruding from his whiskers and his head buried in a book. 'What? Excuse me?' don Daniel would say. Since the other man did not answer more clearly, he would end up walking over to see what he had said.

A new topic had entered the famous conversation, one developed by the doctor alone: he was continually praising don Daniel.

Ever since he had seen the books installed on their shelves and counted for himself the thousands of volumes in don Daniel's library, he could not let ten minutes pass without alluding to his culture, and he was unaware that this had no effect on don Daniel. Don Daniel would answer him evasively, jokingly, making fun of his own erudition.

'What do you expect?' he told the doctor one day to shake off his cloying praise. 'You're born with a fate; think about it.'

I turned my head; don Daniel pointed to a corner of the shelves:

'This is the honeycomb where I buried myself at fourteen.'

The doctor's eyes swelled with admiration like two bubbles.

'Amazing! Amazing!' he repeated for a long time.

Don Daniel had placed his hand on a volume in the bookcase at the back of the room, at about the level of his head. I paid close attention; there were nine volumes the color of coffee with milk.

The next day I got there early and told doña Luisa that I had not been able to study at home. I pounced on the first volume and opened it.

The first page, barely a couple minutes of reading, felt exactly like the end of the world.

I studied the outside of the book and read the title again: *History of Aesthetic Ideas in Spain;* I closed my eyes and kept reading.

If such a thing were possible I would believe I read with my eyes closed, that's how sure I was my efforts were useless.

I have no idea how many pages I managed to get down. I heard footsteps and put the book back in its place; the conversation was already coming up the hall.

Soon afterward, it stationed itself right behind me like a huge darkness, like a storm cloud, and behind it, along the walls, the seven thousand books filled with disdain, filled with evil; all of them were closed, even though they could be opened. Because you're born with a fate, but you have to follow so many leads before you find it!

Any thoughts that tended to lessen my anxiety seemed stupid; the only thing I could think of was to find a sort of tranquillity by remembering comments that had sounded nasty to me when I heard other people make them. Comments my grandmother made that barely hid her desire to criticize: 'This girl talks like a book.' 'This girl is nothing but brains.'

Well, then, I said to myself at that moment, if such is my fate, why is it barred to me?

I did not know why, but the fact is I could not enter.

The words I had tried to get down sat in front of me in that book like a shapeless mass, like mud where I was sinking gradually; nevertheless, I knew others had worked their way through them; that softness, then, that viscousness I felt was not in the ground I was trying to cross but in my own feet.

While I was thinking this, I nibbled on my pen and breathed in the hopeless smell of ink. The desk, the carpet, everything was covered with spots of ink reeking with that smell, a smell every bit as acrid as the one that came from the crib of the gardener's little boy, as unpleasant as if it were caused by the uncertainty and awkwardness of an infant who has just been born but seems to be dying. Because people do not realize that babies struggle with their difficulties; their unsteadiness seems cute when really it's terrible!

Wanting to grab something in your right hand and not being able to touch it, sticking out your arm not quite far enough or reaching too far, rushing forward suddenly and knocking something over, always winding up with your hands in the air, not knowing whether to laugh or cry.

That's exactly what my struggle was like: reading a paragraph and not understanding, backing up, forging ahead and finding a phrase that wobbles because more than half of it is incomprehensible, finding here and there words used every day, and, between some words and others, impassable bridges or dark alleys that even if you get through them leave you with the feeling that you have not.

Why don't they give a person some warning? Their method is to stay on shore; that's how I felt about them standing behind me, waiting to see if I would swim in this muddy water or sink to the bottom.

But they did not even wait there for the results, since they did not know I was engaged in that struggle; they moved on, passed quite close to me, and shut the door.

I went back slowly, like you do when you want to convince yourself that you aren't afraid, picked up the book again, and opened it. Slowly, I forced myself to go slowly, and I moved forward in darkness or in blinding light, but I kept going, without getting confused. Two, three, fifteen yellow pages, with pencil marks in the margins, with some spots that looked like they came from candy, with insects squashed on the pages at the seams. I saw everything because my pace was very deliberate; then I began to read quickly, and I no longer saw any details.

I had the feeling that it was about something familiar. No

landscape was described, and even if there had been I could not have recognized it, since I had never left the province, but I sensed the things discussed were from very close by. What I finally understood was the description of two horses pulling the chariot of the soul. Their features stood out from the pages like one of those paintings that stand out from the frame. One horse was perfect; it was handsomely built and it obeyed the driver's orders. The other was angry and stubborn; its eyes were bloodshot and its mane tangled.

I did not know where I had seen all that before, and in fact I can guarantee that I had never seen it — in the first place, because it was not to be found anywhere. It was like a heavenly vision, but if it was in the sky it must have been in the area that corresponded exactly to the province of Valladolid. I had the impression that I had always seen it painted on our sky like a painting on the ceiling of one of those grand halls filled with judges and officials.

If you could always live under a sky like that you would be in touch with such happiness!

I had seen one, I don't know if it was in the university or City Hall. I remember that I saw it from the doorway of the empty assembly hall. Inside, an employee walked around dusting and there were two cats playing in the feet of the armchairs, and it occurred to me that the halls where they administer justice must be like that one.

I don't know why, but from the door frame, I saw that word outlined nobly, although it was one of the words I usually hated. Whenever I heard others say, 'This is just, this is not just,' I would say to myself: 'A lot I care for your justice.' On the other hand, under a ceiling like that one, the word looked entirely different.

I don't know if these thoughts pulled me out of the book or helped me to enter it. I read only a little bit more, and I had the feeling of having read it all.

From then on, the idea that I could not understand some of the things he said no longer felt humiliating to me. All those things were definitely so lofty that it did not mean defeat if a person took a long time to reach them.

When I left the study, doña Luisa was in the dining room. As I said goodbye I threw my arm around her waist and drew her to the door. We stood there for a while and I wanted to talk about the things I was thinking. As always, though, I did not say anything to her; I hoped that what was in *my* head would travel down my arm, enter through her waist, and find its way up to *her* head. She stared at me after a time and said:

'You've certainly put in a hard afternoon of studying today.'

'How do you know . . . ?' I was going to say doña Luisa, but she looked at me before I finished the *d* and I only said Luisa.

'I don't know, but I know,' she said.

I left then and the next day I went back with my spirit as steady as on the best days. I walked through the streets quickly, feeling that above the thick gray walls of the houses was that blue sky with the two galloping horses. When I got there Luisa was sewing on the right side of the sun porch, don Daniel was reading on the sofa in the study, and the doctor was not there; I could not have asked for anything more.

I opened my books, trying to be quiet so I would not distract him from his reading, but from time to time he said a few words to me. Then he came over to the desk, opened one of the histories, apparently at random, and began to talk about Roman law, this also in a way that seemed totally spontaneous.

Even that topic proved easy for me, although any topic would have proved easy that day.

I listened to him attentively; at the same time, though, with the reflecting that always operates off on its own in a corner of my head, I was thinking about how easily that perfect situation had started up again, and how there was not even a trace of my stupid ambitions or silly ideas left in it.

We were so comfortable at that moment! But I had put the satchel where I kept my papers near the edge of the table, and it fell to the floor when one of the books we were using brushed against it. Since the satchel was unfastened, one of my notebooks slipped out, and out of it slipped a page I had saved, one I tore from my old *Biblical History* before I threw it away.

Don Daniel picked the page up and laid it on the table: the illustration was a picture of the prophet Daniel in the lions' den.

It could not possibly have seemed that the picture just happened to be in my notebook, but if it had been able to seem that way, I would have proved the opposite by blushing until my skin flamed.

Don Daniel acted as if he did not notice, but when I went to put the page back, he moved my hand away, picked up the illustration himself, and stood looking at it for a long, long time.

It was hard to guess from his face what he was thinking: he was scrutinizing the illustration very carefully and I could not imagine what detail he might be uncovering. Finally I saw that he was scrutinizing it in the same careful way you compare a drawing with the model, a thought he confirmed immediately.

'There's a big difference,' he said, looking at me. 'There's an enormous difference, Leticia.'

He lapsed into such a serious silence that I thought he was getting ready to reveal some terrible secret, but he only stressed the same thing again:

'I wish you would realize on your own that there's an enormous difference.'

He saw I was frightened and decided to get us around that awkward situation with a joke.

'My lions will eat me up,' he said, tossing the engraving onto the desk as a way of bringing things to a conclusion.

I took advantage of the opportunity I saw to continue the joke.

'I don't believe it,' I said. 'I'm sure they wouldn't have eaten you either.'

He stopped me:

'I'm not talking about whether they would have eaten me or not; I'm saying that they will eat me.'

He put the page in the history that had been left open, in the section about Roman law, closed the book, and shoved it to one side.

We went back to our studying and he explained something else to me, I don't remember what. Neither of us was much interested, but we both made a big effort to end the lesson on the same note on which it had started.

Suddenly we heard — it might have been audible for a long time, but we both became aware of it at the same instant — music making its way to the study. Luisa was playing upstairs, in the drawing room, but we made no comment. We could have said, 'How well she plays,' or simply, 'She's playing,' because it was something that did not usually happen, but we made no comment and this made the incident even more serious.

I saw that don Daniel was waiting for me to say I wanted to go up and be with her. I did not hide the fact that I was listening; I made him wait for a long time before I asked if we could end the lesson. I did not pick up on the way he introduced topics that could as easily have been drawn out as cut short. 'Well, we'll have to talk about this at length,' he would say suddenly, lapsing into silence to see if I took advantage of it, but I let the silence remain empty — in other words, full of the music coming down from the drawing room — until the music stopped; Luisa could not stand that solitude for very long. I heard her mules on the stairs.

A little while later, don Daniel ended the lesson and I left as if nothing had happened.

I thought she had probably done it only to escape her boredom for a while, but that was not the case: Luisa kept playing day after day at the same time we had our lessons, and I continued to say nothing about it and to have no idea that she also played when I was not there.

One morning I went out to buy something or other and when I crossed the plaza I heard her piano from a distance.

I heard it and did not believe it; I went closer; it was a little after twelve, the sun was directly overhead, and she was playing endlessly.

She was not playing Adriana's pieces; this was something different. My ear was accustomed by then to music that arranges the notes in something like necklaces, and I thought I knew the garlands it made with all their many variations. On the other hand, this music described a new curve; it was more languid, although it too was very beautiful.

I thought about this as I walked and about how it all held a mystery; soon I was tiptoeing up the stairs.

I stopped at the door to the drawing room, which was half closed, and when she finished I made a slight noise. She turned her head.

'I could hear you from far away,' I said.

Luisa moved her eyebrows in a way that meant I had done the right thing by coming. She waited a minute for me to ask a question and immediately decided to say something that did not provide an answer to what I planned to ask, since it was an explanation.

'A person's fingers get all rusty if they don't get to practice,' she said, looking at her hands.

'Your playing was wonderful,' I told her.

'Oh no, not yet,' she answered, 'although it might be more accurate to say not any longer.'

Grabbing the seat on the piano stool with both hands, she rested the tips of her feet on the floor and made the stool turn until the screw was completely unthreaded; then she raised her legs and let herself spin down, whirling around rapidly. She spun like that so she could take her time deciding whether or not to tell me her secret. But we heard don Daniel's footsteps below and went out to the stairway.

When don Daniel saw us together, he thought he had found the explanation for my silence during the afternoons, thinking that I went during the mornings to keep Luisa company while she practiced. To me he said nothing, but he asked her a question right away:

'How's it coming? Are you making any progress?'

'Little by little,' she said.

I realized then not how they were talking but that they were talking; it had been some time since I heard a single word pass between them.

I analyzed those two sentences thoroughly, but I learned nothing from them; all I managed to do was push the mystery of the music into the background.

At home, during dinner, I was thinking the whole time about whether there might be silence between them like the one that usually prevailed in our dining room. Of course the children were always there, shouting and getting into things, but I was sure they sat through it all without saying a word.

In the two sentences I had heard I was determined to find something like the key to all the sentences that might pass between them, and I thought I could see those sentences, without suspecting, of course, what words they were made of. All I saw was don Daniel's dry terseness as he spit out his sentences and Luisa's timid firmness as she answered.

A new dialogue just like the other one, I thought, might be brewing at that moment, breaking the silence that floated above the plates and wineglasses.

I remembered perfectly the smell of what they were having

for dinner that day, which was the main reason I could feel I was in their dining room and imagine their dialogue or their silence. The smell of their kitchen was so wonderful it was irresistible and you could never compare it with the smell of the kitchen in my house. Something marvelous was always floating from it: a subtle spice or the steam that trails behind things when they emerge from the oven all golden brown.

As I had walked down the stairs, my imagination was still working on Luisa's secret; then don Daniel spit out that sentence just as I was going to say: 'Something smells divine all the way out here!' That would have been enough for Luisa to insist that I stay and I could have seen if they talked and, if they talked, how they talked.

Silently, the way meals were served every day at our house, my aunt put a huge piece of stewed chicken on my plate; I downed it in four mouthfuls and she gave me another helping with lots of different things. When she saw I made no effort to restrain her, she exclaimed:

'My Lord, what a way to eat; I've never seen anything like it.'

My aunt did not understand that nothing could have satisfied the hunger I felt at that moment.

Anyone else as anguished as I was would probably not have been able to swallow a crumb of bread. I felt a kind of impatience choking me and I devoured everything in front of me as if that would put an end to it. Because suddenly it seemed to me that the first thing that needed to be done was to put an end to something, make something change, or make something, anything, happen.

So what if my father and aunt had decided to let themselves slowly waste away; no one could stop them. Luisa had her music, don Daniel had his books and his conversation. I had them, it was true, but I needed to be able at least to tell one day in Simancas from the rest.

When they no longer put any more food within my reach, I kept looking for crumbs on the tablecloth and thinking how the anxiety attacking me was some meaningless thing I could not communicate to anyone, and if I did communicate it, no one would understand it or support me while I fought it. This feeling was so strong there was something impetuous or provocative about it. I would have liked to shout about all that, throw it in someone's face, maybe because I felt that I could make something spring forth from the darkness, that something was brewing behind my back.

I said nothing. Two or three lessons followed about subjects as impenetrable as rocks, with no lapse in either the rigor of the explanation or the intensity of the attention paid to it. Upstairs, those strains of music, like a natural phenomenon, like the wind when it whistles in the chimney.

The fourth day, I arrived and found the house seemingly deserted, but since everything was open I realized that some one must be close by. I started to work in the study; in a short while I heard footsteps, and Luisa appeared at the door.

She came in and rested her elbows on a stack of books on the desk, letting both her hands hang in front of me.

Her hands were transfigured.

It seemed impossible that those hands in front of my eyes had ever plunged into floury dough, that they had hammered, adjusted screws, unrolled sticky splicing tape. At that moment her hands were pure spirit.

Besides her wedding band she was wearing a ring she always wore, a small narrow circle of turquoises. The blue varied in color, becoming more greenish in some stones, the ones that looked mottled, that people call impure. This made the ring look like something so alive it seemed to be more a vein than a ring: it was exactly the color of the veins showing through the back of her hand.

'I . . . ,' I started to say.

'You know . . . ,' Luisa said at precisely the same instant. We both stopped talking at once, and right away started to argue about which of us should speak first. Finally she gave in.

'I was going to ask you,' she said, 'if you know that next month marks the teacher's twenty-fifth anniversary at her school.'

'How could that be, when she seems so young?'

'About sixty,' Luisa said. 'She deserves a real tribute, don't you think? It will take place the first of September, which was her first day at the school.'

She immediately began to tell me that the mayor had come to read her a letter from the ladies in the charitable organization that had paid for the teacher's studies. They were asking the women of Simancas to help with the celebration they planned in her honor. The teacher was the first poor young woman they had helped, and they wanted to commemorate her twenty-five years of virtue as their society's greatest triumph.

While Luisa told me all this I was smiling, because I remembered that a few days before I had seen the mayor leaving our house as I got home and noticed that he stood against the doorway chatting with my aunt for a long time.

'What was he talking to you about?' I had asked my aunt.

'Nothing, just nonsense,' had been her response.

I told Luisa this, and she seemed a bit flustered.

'Well,' she said, 'my answer was that these two hands will do everything they can.'

'That's the only answer you could have given,' I told her. 'But do you know everything those hands can do?'

'No. What can they do?'

Her innocent expression made me laugh so hard I could not answer.

'Oh!' she exclaimed. 'What was it you were going to say before?'

'I was going to say, the truth is I was going to say that I would like to see what one of your hands would do with a sword.'

'A sword?'

'Yes. I have watched your hands do so many things, but suddenly it occurred to me there was something else I needed to see: that's what it was, the shining sword people talk about. I would like to see one of your hands grasp that sword by its gold hilt, right at the crosspiece, and raise it high in the air.'

I went on with some nonsense or other about the archangel Michael and I saw that the way I was idealizing Luisa's hands was making her withdraw. She cringed in fear, and she was almost trembling, but the fact is she was like I had seen her at other times, not frightened but disoriented and indecisive, not sure how to react, not sure if she even wanted to react.

Finally, with one of those sighs a person breathes in by drawing air through the nose, she shook off her uncertainty.

'What a featherbrain,' she said, reaching out a hand and giving me a good slap on the forehead.

I had been concentrating so hard on my thoughts about her hands that I could have kissed the one that slapped me, but it escaped: don Daniel was in the doorway.

He came toward the desk, sat down in his chair, and gave me a smile that seemed strange and . . . I cannot help adding another adjective: cruel.

'You're in an epic mood today, aren't you?' he started out by remarking.

I made no answer. He kept on:

'I think you'd find the story of Alexander the Great like a nursery tale today.'

I could not answer.

'A glimpse at the rule of three would be better,' he said. 'It steadies the nerves more.'

'Much more,' I finally answered, with a completely serene voice.

Several days later, don Daniel came out with another sarcastic remark when he found us together, absorbed in our sewing. 'That thing's going to be more of a gala than a tribute.'

Luisa and I were silent; now it was his turn to get no response.

I put what I was sewing on the table and went into the study. I had made a real effort to study more than ever, even though I was spending long hours with the girls, working at one of their houses, so they could finish the handiwork for their exhibit, and then I was working with Luisa on my dress for the celebration and on the part assigned to me, because I thought I could manage to do everything, and in fact I could.

That effort diminished neither my attention nor my intelligence. What happened was that don Daniel began to alter his technique: before, he had done nothing more than teach me what I already knew, and this became clear to me at that moment. The base of all his explanations had invariably been central points I knew thoroughly; he added branches to my knowledge, which meant there was an essence running through all of them that was never foreign to me. Suddenly he changed, although not openly. He gave me no chance to ask him why things were different, and, on top of it, if I had tried to prove that I noticed the difference I could not have pointed to what it consisted of. The thing is that when everything seemed to be going along as usual, with one clause he would tackle subjects I knew nothing about, without giving me any warning, as if it were to be taken for granted that we had always set those subjects aside because he was so agreeable or, rather, because they were so complicated he was sure I would not be able to figure them out. When he tackled them, he always did it with a phrase so clear, precise, and complex that in one instant he projected in front of me the whole scope of my ignorance. The phrase was never either an explanation nor a blunt question, because that would have given away his new tactics: it was usually an allusion to things a lot could have been said about and things there was not even any reason to ask about.

I had enough willpower not to let him see how flustered I was, but I walked home carrying all those enigmas inside of me, as irremediably as someone who has swallowed a poison and knows there is no way to get rid of it or keep it from invading the body little by little.

The effect of those words was truly lethal, because they created a void where everything seemed nullified. The words were clearly marked in my brain, but like figures cut from a piece of paper; their entire space was a hollow, and all my other faculties peered into it, in fascination, about to be swallowed up.

Suddenly, when there was nothing left for my memory to do in the sphere of intelligence, it would bring to the forefront a feeling or a type of passion. I say a type, because it was a type of bad passion, also mixed with good: something like an ambition, a revenge, and a tantalizing dream all at the same time. Then I would pounce on my book with the poem I had chosen to recite at the celebration and read the poem a couple of times. After that I would repeat it tirelessly in the dark, although I knew it by heart; I would not miss a comma, but mentally I practiced the inflections I would put in my voice and the pauses or the animation I needed to add to certain passages.

I never dared to recite it out loud; even so, I was sure it would be perfect.

Sometimes I had spoken a couple of lines in my room but I had stopped immediately, from a kind of embarrassment at saying them in front of the mirror on my wardrobe, where I could see the reflection of my bed, the clothes rack, and the sink, and especially where I could see myself reflected like that, wearing an ordinary dress, so different from the way things would have to be, from what I would have to achieve the day of the celebration.

I had recited only a few sections for Luisa; apparently she had never read the poem, and I never left the book for her. I gave her a general description and she told me it sounded wonderful before she heard me.

The most difficult thing was convincing the Organizing Committee to accept our plan.

One afternoon, the mayor gathered everyone together and there was unanimous acceptance of what they proposed for the first half of the day: the Mass, the handiwork exhibit, the banquet for important people.

Then they began to discuss the formal celebration that would take place at City Hall in the late afternoon.

They all agreed that those formalities should last only a short time, but they wanted to cram so many things into the time it seemed bound to stretch on forever.

Luisa had insisted on taking me with her to that meeting, because she said it would help muster her courage when it was time to speak. In fact, she did participate with great self-assurance.

She started by saying that she wanted to do something by herself because she was not a native of Simancas, although she could not be considered exactly an outsider either. What she offered was to play some Chopin waltzes, which would make the celebration more festive.

'Good,' the mayor said right away, 'very good. We can't have a party without music, and I don't think the band is appropriate, since this celebration is for a woman.'

Everyone agreed.

'Leticia, Colonel Valle's little girl, is in a similar position,' Luisa added. 'She did not begin her studies here with the teacher, but she has received some instruction from her, and more important, she is very fond of her. She can recite some poetry in her honor.'

Very good! everyone said once again.

'It would be nice if she recited some poetry written especially for the occasion,' the doctor added.

Luisa cut him off:

'Who would write it?' She did not think he would have the courage to answer, but in case he did, she added, without giving him time to take a breath: 'There is no writer here of that stature. It's better for her to select something by a great local poet; she'll recite a poem by Zorrilla.'

'That's ridiculous,' the doctor exclaimed. His own outburst must have frightened him, and he added: 'You know, doña Luisa, Zorrilla is a poet who no longer interests anyone!'

'You won't deny that he's a great poet.'

'A great versifier, madam, which is not the same thing.'

The discussion went on forever. The mayor did not venture to impose his own criterion, because he did not have one, and he looked out into space above the heads of the others. He was looking way into the distance; I think he had mentally transported himself to the main promenade through the gardens in Valladolid, which runs from the statue of Columbus at one edge of the park to the statue of Zorrilla at the other. Since he knew well how courageous a figure Columbus had been, he felt sure that the man at the opposite end of the promenade would also have to be someone important. Finally he intervened, reminded them all to act like gentlemen, and sided with Luisa.

Everything was settled just as the two of us had planned.

A feverish week followed: mornings and afternoons I embroidered at school with the girls and then I ran to Luisa's house. I had taken her the dress I wore for my first communion and, between the two of us, we were transforming it a bit: skirt let down to my ankles, sash wrapped tight at the waist, collar gone, and sleeves gathered at the forearm with an elastic band.

'Why do you insist on putting elastic in them?' Luisa asked me.

'Now you'll know my trick,' I confessed to her. 'My aunt won't let me wear sleeves that are really short.'

Late in the afternoon, my torture would begin. Don Daniel's smile had frozen on his mouth, and it remained unchanged, neither waning nor widening as he walked through the house. More than a smile, it was an indescribable way of showing his teeth: it was the smile of a wolf.

It is easy to imagine that if a wolf smiled it would smile like he did, but the thing is, if a wolf were to put its hands in its pants pockets, it would also do that just like he did; just like he did, it would lean on the door frames, or walk through the house without uttering a word.

What was much worse than anything a wolf could do were the little quips he would come out with from time to time.

'You look terribly tired today,' Luisa had the bright idea to remark one afternoon as I stood up to go into the study.

'It would be better,' don Daniel added, 'for you to give up studying until the two of you finish preparing for the ninth Olympics.'

I left then, saying that in fact I felt exhausted, and I went out into the street, although I did not go home. I turned down a little alley to the left and I heard the bell from the church of the Arrabal; that's the direction I headed. There were a lot of women going in for the novena. I walked more slowly until they all went in; only one beggar woman with her dog stayed behind in the doorway, but at last she went in as well.

I got to the hermitage and walked around it until I was all the way in the back, all the way to the apse; from there you could barely hear the murmuring inside. The solitude was wonderful. Not a single figure was visible on the entire hillside; the sun had set, but the light was so clear you could count the haystacks left from the harvest.

The silence was total. I coughed a little to see if there would be much of an echo: not a trace. If I had shouted, the sound would have been lost on the plain immediately, but if I spoke in a low voice it was possible to gauge just the right tone, and I was certain my words would not carry inside the church.

I recited the whole poem. The four hundred forty-eight lines stretched into space exactly as the author had imagined them: they formed a great road, wide at the beginning, and at the end like a very thin thread.

The poem was 'The Race,' that legend about the Moorish king whose runaway horse carries him to paradise, and there, in such perfect peace, I convinced myself that it would turn out beautifully. The sublime figure escaping from earth would spring from my words, and from time to time I would extend one arm, not marking anything in particular, but suggesting with my open hand, among the rows of dignitaries, a figure every bit as superior as the figure of one of those fictional characters marked by a unique destiny.

I was sure I would achieve the effect I wanted, because my voice was the only thing about my whole person that I considered truly satisfactory, and my diction was so perfect that even the villagers were always praising me for it.

I felt less sure about the general impression I would create, my dress, and the way I would place my feet. I could not see myself in a mirror there, although I sensed I was all right.

Suddenly the beggar woman's dog appeared and walked up to me, hoping I would pet him, but I did not stop; I kept on reciting and I stared at the dog. That upset him, and he went off with his head down.

I stayed there a long time, until it got dark and I started to feel afraid. I decided to go in, but the prayers were over and people were already coming out. I walked into the crowd and no one realized where I had come from.

I did not think anything could happen on the morning of that day: I was absent, with my thoughts fixed on five o'clock, which had to come. At ten o'clock, though, cars from Valladolid began to appear in the plaza, and in one of them, the one I felt least curious about because it was filled with the most venerable ladies from the charitable society, my professor turned up.

When I saw her sleek figure, with her tight-fitting gray tailored suit, among that heap of huge black skirts, I felt as though I were losing my bearings, my balance, my center of gravity for the entire day.

I would have liked to hide; I would also have liked it if Luisa had been near me so I could squeeze her arm and exchange glances with her, but she was with my aunt, who had felt obliged to go to church, and I was waiting until my aunt went home so I could join the group walking toward the school. I saw her and felt my feet rooted to the ground.

My aunt saw her too.

'We should go and say hello,' she said.

I suggested that it would be better to wait until she was not surrounded by so many people. Of course that seemed like a great suggestion to my aunt.

I stood there thinking. Luisa was walking with the teacher now, and I saw her looking all around for me. She could not understand why I was not with them, but I wanted to get my thoughts straight.

Finally, my professor saw us from a distance and we walked to meet her halfway.

'This girl has certainly grown!' she said, putting a hand on my shoulder.

Her voice seemed very cold to me. She had always treated me

like you treat a boy, but before, in Valladolid, that seemed like her style or, rather, like a game we had agreed on. On this occasion it struck me as nothing more than a wall, a restraint, because I could no longer participate in the game.

My aunt started to chat with her; she's the only person I have seen my aunt speak to naturally. I escaped: I'd had enough.

I ran toward the school, where they were getting everything ready for the arrival of the ladies from the commission. Luisa questioned me with her eyes, and I made a gesture as if I were escaping from some dreadful torture. 'My aunt . . . ,' I said, and nothing more. That way Luisa could think we'd had one of those unpleasant scenes, nothing really important . . .

I did not know how to tell her about my encounter. I had talked to her about my professor so many times, with all the enthusiasm I felt when I remembered her, and at that moment I found it immensely painful that she might see her so distanced from me and realize that this could influence my mood and cause me to make a fool of myself in the afternoon. But it was inevitable that the two of us would be left more or less by ourselves and that we could talk about whatever we wanted, because we began to arrange a long table where the handiwork was displayed. The table had been made by pushing desks together and covering them with white sheets, and we began to thumbtack a red and yellow ribbon to it, making garlands around the edges, with bows on the corners.

I felt miserable because it was impossible to tell Luisa I thought all that looked horrible. Horrible is not the word: disastrous.

If my professor had not turned up there, I would not have noticed it, but knowing that her eyes would pass over all those things depressed me so much I was left without a drop of energy.

My despair must have been so evident that Luisa finally asked me:

'What's wrong?'

At that moment the ladies were approaching the door of the school, and with my professor, very much apart from the group, clutching her arm and whispering in her ear, came my aunt.

I made up some absurd explanation having to do with their arrival, so absurd I cannot even remember it: something about no longer having any freedom to do anything.

Luisa begged me to stay calm, and I promised her that I would. To pretend that I was, I left, letting things go on around me as if I could not see them, and what went on were those greetings, those congratulations, that praise.

Finally everyone went to the banquet and I went home with my aunt.

The table was already set. When we sat down, my aunt said in that impersonal way they had of talking at my house, as if she were speaking to someone you could not be sure was there, just like that, just in case the person might be present . . . :

'Who turned up there, among all those saintly dames from the commission but Margarita Velayos.'

My father raised his eyebrows and smiled:

'Margarita; well, what do you know.'

'She said she'll come by for a minute to see you when she leaves the banquet,' my aunt added.

'I don't know why she would have come here, with all these yokels,' she said, as if musing to herself.

No one said anything else, but for a long time my father's expression looked softer.

On my bed I had laid out my dress, my belt, and the ribbon I was going to wear in my hair; I thought I had already spent two hours or more getting ready, but I could not find the resolve to put those things on, even though it was getting late. I knew that my professor was going to come and I did not like the thought of having to talk to her about what I was going to do.

I walked around my room for a long time, not being able to decide on a pose, not even thinking about the poem, paying attention to nothing except the noises that came from the doorway below. Finally I heard the door open and her voice and my aunt's; I went down.

When I went into my father's room, my professor was sitting on a low chair next to the armchair. There was a silence as if they were never going to start talking. Finally my aunt decided to speak:

'How was the banquet?'

'The worst thing was the coffee,' my professor answered, shrugging her shoulders.

'That can be fixed with a *good* cup,' my aunt said and left the room.

Not a word more; the two of them sat there in an agreeable silence, without a bit of violence. It was clear that if they were quiet it was not because they could not speak, but because they did not need to, as if each one knew everything about the other, as if she were the visitor for whom nothing would be news.

I had positioned myself with my back to the balcony, leaning against the iron fastening on the window; watching them, I remembered those strained tales my father usually paralyzed company with. The camp, the jackals, the dog, the background, black as night, of a scheme there was no way to fathom.

What was happening at that moment did not mean those things had been forgotten but quite the opposite; those things were unspoken because they both knew them.

Sitting there with her knee almost touching my father's, Margarita Velayos was like an officer who had fought with him, who had explored those shadowy outposts with him, who had seen him fall and was the only person who knew the face of the one who had wounded him.

They had coffee. She drank her glass of cognac in three sips:

three small sips, but sips that were taken slowly, with the glass cradled in her hand the way smokers hold a pipe. At the same time, though, as she made that masculine gesture, her head tilted forward as daintily as a virgin's.

She had a sharp, flawless profile, dark skin, and straight, very dark hair that fell naturally in *bandeaux* alongside her face. The rest of it she gathered at the nape of her neck in a small silky chignon that hung beneath her straw hat.

She was so noble that her contradictions had been refined and elevated until they seemed incorruptible in the aura of cold emanating from her.

While I watched her I felt a terrible pain in my back. The bolt on the balcony window was boring into my spine, and I pressed all my weight against it, trying to use that pain to control the whirl of discordant impulses churning inside me.

When she left, my father held her hand for a long time.

'This has brought me enormous happiness,' was all he said.

He looked at her with immense sorrow, as if to let her see such infinite sorrow so she would be able to gauge the immensity of his happiness.

I did get to the celebration. I got there with my dress on, my hair fixed, and everything set on the outside; no one knew my spirits were shattered.

I went with my aunt, whom I encouraged to go with me. Luisa and I had agreed to go together, but I had already taken care of things with her in the morning, telling her it would be impossible for me to get out of going with my family, and she was not surprised. That way I still had an excuse that accounted for my despair and explained my mistakes. Once I was there, though, I could not keep to myself any longer; people were all finding someone they wanted to be with. Luisa arrived with don Daniel, but they separated right away and she came to look for me; she assumed I was waiting for her help.

We sat together. I don't know who was near us, I don't know how it all started. Speeches, applause, speeches.

The room was full; a lot of children had come by bus from the schools in Valladolid and they were buzzing around like a swarm of bees. It was inconceivable that one voice, one lone voice, could manage to be heard over that hum, and I did not want to think about my voice needing to project itself in just a little while.

Two or three times a doubt crossed my mind about whether or not I would remember the poem; mentally, I outlined the first stanza and immediately pushed it away with a kind of re-pugnance. I had written the poem on a piece of paper, but I felt I would probably not even be able to think clearly enough to read it and I concentrated on the way I should unroll the long strip where I had written the words, holding it with just one hand.

I had copied the poem in very small letters on a strip of parchmentlike paper, and when I held the strip unrolled it would form a spiral on each end.

I had practiced until the position of my left hand was perfect, because it was the hand I would use to hold the paper. Before that I had spent hours, even days, solving the geometrical puzzle that would let me have a spiral on each side; if the strip were simply rolled up, it would form a *C* as I unwound it, and what I wanted was for it to form an *S*. This meant I had to fold the strip in half, so that once it was open the two halves would unroll on either side of each other.

For a long time my imagination took refuge in this idea, and while I thought about it I would wind the roll of paper too tight. Then I would be afraid the paper had gotten twisted and would not work on its own when I unrolled it. I would loosen it, leave it open for a while, and then fix it again.

The speeches were given on the large platform where they had placed the speakers' table. Luisa's piano was on the right, and on the left there was a small half circle formed by pots of laurel where people would stand when they recited.

A group of boys went up first. The teacher had taught them a scene from some drama where a man was dying and falling dramatically to the floor, hitting his head on the stage. It was really embarrassing!

Luisa's arm, which had been linked through mine, slid under it. I looked at her and saw she was starting to take off her hat, which told me she was going to perform. It was a large, dark straw picture hat, anchored with pins; she put it on her lap and shook her curls, although the weight did not seem to have flattened them.

The mayor announced her performance, rummaging for phrases and piling one on top of the other in an attempt to make her contribution seem appropriate. Hers was a tribute of friendship, he said, the best bouquet of flowers; it made your hair stand on end to hear him.

As soon as she had slid her arm under mine, Luisa got up from the chair where she was sitting, left her hat on the seat, and walked toward the three steps in front of the piano. I noticed then that the dress she had on was one I had not seen before, and I had not made even the slightest comment. The fabric was printed in shades of dry leaves, and she wore a long amethyst-colored necklace that hung to her waist. She looked radiant as she went up the steps to the platform.

Her music filled the room, as always. I forgot all the uneasiness I had felt, because anything ugly dissolved in the solitude emanating from the majesty of that music.

Listening, you had to forget the rest of the universe and feel alone with it, the way it was in the solitude of her drawing room, or the way its chords reached me from a distance as I walked along the street, when everything seemed hypnotized, with the world condensed in a corner or a stone on the sidewalk.

When she finished there was a lengthy and prolonged storm of applause, which died down and then rose up many times, because they wanted her to play an encore. Just as some of the applause would stop, some would start again, in real disagreement; this left the audience expecting something but not knowing what it was, like when a flock of pigeons passes overhead, endlessly flying away and returning, and you don't know where it will light.

Until then I felt as though I were in a kind of ecstasy, but suddenly I was plunged into confusion as if I sensed something chasing me, fated to rush after me: the mayor's words, in which I could make out something like 'The composition of that incomparable poet . . .'

My path crossed Luisa's in front of the platform and I squeezed her hand. I went up, and made a curtsy in front of the table. The mayor pointed out the half circle of laurels.

'Stand over there, where they can see you easily,' he told me quickly in a low voice.

The fact that the mayor found me worthy of being seen meant nothing: nevertheless, when I reached the laurels — the journey had seemed like a mile — I was almost serene, because as I passed in front of the table I automatically looked up at Alfonso XIII whose portrait hung on the scarlet velvet that formed the canopy. I was walking quickly, but it seemed to me that in the rapid glance I gave him his arrogant expression turned into a happy-go-lucky smile. He was portrayed standing, with one hand holding his shako and the other resting on the hilt of his saber, and it seemed to me that he raised his shoulders with the same gesture I had seen Mr. Marcos's son make under my balcony. I seemed to hear his unforgettable phrase, 'Whatever you want, baby,' and I felt that victory had been conceded to me in advance, that everything would turn out the way I wanted; I unfolded the paper and began to recite.

It is always difficult to gauge how much breath to give the first line, but this is especially true for 'The Race,' because the poem bolts off in the first words with the momentum of a horse defying the bit.

In the first four Alexandrines my voice already sounded like a gallop to me, and I immediately forced myself to soften what I had heard the doctor call onomatopoeic monotony: that was not difficult. After the suggestion of the horse's impetuousness comes the description of the wild images passing alongside the Moorish king. The rhythm can be less accentuated then, and the words can be emphasized, since they are so beautiful in themselves:

From the white poplar the branches extended,
the tops there so airy of palm trees and pines,
the scramble of hawthorns and blackberry vines,
the ivy hanging from boulders all jagged.

I extended my right arm with a vague motion. Before walking to the platform I had surreptitiously rolled my sleeves up to the shoulder. Although my arms were extremely thin, they were not unpoetic because my bones did not stick out at the joints. That meant I could use them to gesticulate poetically, and I turned a little on my heels then, as if to direct my motions toward the back of the hall.

In the first octave, as I alluded to the figure of the hero, barely mentioning the actual rider tossed by the impetuous movement of the horse, I looked toward the speakers' table, putting in my expression nothing more than the passive precision you would use to tell about an event that happened long ago. Then I directed my gestures at the entire audience, when I began to allude to the images and monsters filling the king's delirium as he raced along, as if they were beginning to appear there, and at a certain moment, after repeating several times that the images were passing in such and such a way, as I said again:

Passing they were as Al-hamar saw them
pass by not knowing how quickly they went . . .

I stretched out my arm toward a particular spot, exactly as I had practiced behind the church. With my hand open, I pointed to a place in the front row of spectators, as if to touch something with the tips of my fingers, as if I were drawing back a veil and disclosing the mystery. And from there, right from the platform, I could hear his heart beating.

This is not just words: I felt it.

For the same reason, my innate faculties were almost obliterated: I was looking and not seeing.

The murmur and the restlessness of the crowd, everything had been erased, including the distance of five or six meters that separated me from don Daniel.

Logically, it was impossible that I could hear his heart from where I was, and it was also outside of any logic that he would start at the name of king Al-hamar, as if he had heard his own name. It happened, though: at that moment there was no distance and there were no secrets between him and me.

He saw the ideas thronging in my head the way I saw how the blood coursed faster in his veins, because the poem also helped me discover that or provoke it, I'm not sure which. In addition, there was an allusion to the agitation felt by the rider as he rode beyond the realm of the logical.

I made another gesture of emphasis with my arm outstretched again in the same direction:

In his temples a gallop did pound
of blood that beat so violent and loud
'til rang his ears with deafening sound
of pitch so deep and pace dully slow.

But I did not simply want to torment him, and besides, why should he have felt tormented by that? It's impossible to explain. What I can say for certain is that he was really tortured then and that the possibility of being able to make him suffer had figured in my plans from the beginning.

I have talked about this before, about vengeance. Of course there was vengeance, and what proves it was fair is the way his eyes got that dark expression immediately, the one that seemed about to unleash some terrible catastrophe at any moment. Exactly like the day the picture of the prophet Daniel slipped out of my papers.

Except that now I was the one showing him the image from the platform, with all my daring, because he could not silence me or make me change the subject.

His paleness, the shadows cast by the lights in the room on the circles under his eyes, I don't know if they awakened in me a wave of tenderness or of fear; but I went on because the sonority of those lines carried me along and because I wanted to finish. Although there was no finish, I mean there was no real finality.

It all led to nothing, and there was no ending that might have amounted to some kind of proof. No, there was only the vertigo of accumulating things, of mentioning them, of surrounding and decorating the chosen figure with every beautiful object from heaven and earth. And there was the fact of naming those things, which was enhanced then by the syllables, not by the words, by truly celestial sounds with such pure nuances of meaning they created the sensation of leaving the material realm behind.

So when the king thinks he is going to repeat 'the Prophet's dark, mystic journey' there are sentences that sparkle like this one:

Stars he glimpsed hung in suspense
on such gold they were enchained;

in them o'er the darkness reigned
spirits lighting all with truth.

Unfortunately, though, the consonant is off here. I cannot understand how such a skillful writer could be so weak he would use a provincialism like that; how, after lines like those, he could continue with:

Spirits seeming so immense
some in shapes of cocks and deer
horses, too, in forms quite clear
of an awesome magnitude.

You can tell that when he was little they let him say *magnituth* at home, the way uneducated people talk in Valladolid. I find this intolerable, and I had to work really hard to hide the lameness in that rhyme.

Anything rather than say *magnituth*, but if I had said *magnitud*, letting the *d* sound, the lack of agreement would have been too evident; so I chose to say *magnitú*, drawing out the *u* with a little trick.

That ruse came out as spontaneously as everyone from the city says *Valladolí*. We don't want to say *Valladolith*, like common people, and we don't want to accentuate the *d* because it would seem affected. So we suppress the consonant like that, quite naturally.

I don't know if it was the influence of that defect, which seemed to reach immense proportions when I heard it in public; the thing is I began to feel an anguished uncertainty about the beauty of the poem.

I kept on with the description of the visions and realized that suddenly I was saying

Grottoes picturesque he saw
and the sylphs who lived therein.

Picturesque! The truth is, the word is horrible.

Could that be what the doctor was referring to, when he said the poem could no longer interest anyone?

I did not dare look at where he was sitting. I kept going; at the end there would be another portrait of the king as he is about to ride into the region entered only by the chosen, as he faces the narrow path stretched waveringly ahead:

So very fine
as that thin thread
from which do hang
their own sure line
caterpillars.

I felt sure of myself again, and again I entered the hero's domain, his dark mystique, this time with the quickened pace of the verse, which emphasizes the feeling of risk so well:

It is the bridge,
the one of life
that everyone
here born in strife
will meet and cringe
and surely cross.

I kept on for a long while without making any further mental comments, forgetting myself to the point that I no longer recognized my own voice. If the poem was onomatopoeic, my voice identified with its nuances like a chameleon. In my voice, the poem bubbled like the tossing of turbulent waters:

How frightening:
eyes black as tar,
mouth whitening,
the horse a flash,
frothing and proud;

each step a lash,
it bellows loud,
the bridge does crash
then rears and bawls
as if to spar;
beneath, a swell
the waves wild are.
Israfel
stands there so tall
to watch who goes
and does not fall,
for well he knows
the ride to jar,
the bridge to bar
the infidel;
and now he waits
and watches well;
his eyes roam far
the steed to tell
of Al-hamar.

There was a huge silence. Maybe among the adults it was only from politeness, but the children did not stir because they were following the story with every one of their five senses. Perhaps it was clearer for them than for anyone: they saw it, they followed it with their eyes.

I pointed to the back of the room as if it were way off in the distance:

He comes, draws near,
so swift and clear,
so fast his race
so soon in space
finds he is hung;

the bridge now quakes,
he too is swung
as turbulent
the ocean breaks
and turgidly
the waves are flung,
their roaring clear
to sea and star.
By terror stung,
his gaze cast far,
water so wild
his eye forsakes,
for he does fear
the sight would mar
courage sans par;
and so he takes
no breath nor thought
of that air drear
in his throat caught,
since heaven and earth
will help him not . . .

More serenely now, as if inspired by the certainty of the poem's glorious finish, as if the king were beginning to step on the solid ground of his own virtues. Pointing again to the first row of seats:

He rides with speed,
just knight since birth,
brave king who makes
decisions stern
but always wakes
respect in turn,
high place to earn,

his house he leads:
the first Nazar.

He blinked, as if he had suddenly felt something touch his eyelids. From the way he shook his lashes, I could tell he was refusing the words I had sent with all my strength: 'the first!'

At that moment, my voice would have been the envy of any general who ever led a battle. And he had to be quiet. He could not say: 'There's a big difference, there's an enormous difference.'

Suddenly I thought: 'Luisa. What will she say? What would she say, if she could say something now?'

I looked at her. At first all I could see was a blur of gold where her amethyst necklace was shining; finally, I managed to make out the radiance of her face.

She would not say anything, because she had no thoughts, although this does not mean she had no feelings: she felt my success. The fact that she too had been successful made no difference to her: she had done it all for me. If she had acted only from kindness, though, what she did would have impressed me less. Deep down, it was much more complicated. Luisa wanted me to fulfill my ambitions almost as much as I did myself; she needed to see that I did what I wanted, that I did it well, and that she could say, 'It was just perfect.'

Her serenity bolstered my courage and I bolted enthusiastically toward the end. Onto that shaky bridge.

Thoughts reeling,
and feeling
demented,
revealing
his terror,
the far side
he now gains;

128

quick to face,
he'll not hide,
the short race
that remains,
with valor!
and courage!

Very difficult, because my breathing was agitated now, not only from ten minutes of recitation, but from living the poem, from pronouncing the last words precisely, since the monosyllabic lines are lost if even one vowel is blurred:

A leap,
so steep
he takes.
A dare
cross deep
he makes,
then keeps.
Safe!
Free
there,
waits;
breaks
flees
where?

They applauded, although I don't know if it was a lot or a little because everything turned into a blur as I spoke the last line. I passed from one pair of hands to the next until I had made the rounds of all the honored guests at the speakers' table. The women hugged me, the men patted me on the cheeks. I must have looked like a crazy woman, because I managed to smile, but I felt that I hated everyone.

When I hugged the teacher I rested my cheek against hers and felt her face wet with tears. She held me tight for a long time against her generous breasts, and I almost burst into tears myself, but I refused to succumb. As I walked down from the platform I continued to give out, equally, smiles and savage looks until I was back with Luisa. I sat down beside her again, linked her arm through mine once more, and stopped thinking. I believed I felt at peace, as if I were a hundred miles from everything, until the celebration was over.

From where I was sitting I noticed that don Daniel's chair was empty and I found it impossible that he would have left. When we got up, I saw him walking toward the exit with the doctor; I made sure they did not see me.

When I put on my coat I realized that I was trembling. They had opened the doors and let in a bitter cold. I finished my goodbyes in a hurry because I wanted to plunge into that cold. I said goodbye to Luisa and left with my aunt, prying her from the group around Margarita Velayos, who told me goodbye in the same icy way she had said hello. The women with her were no doubt talking about me, because I heard her say,

'She always did have a prodigious memory.'

Home with my aunt. I watched her out of the corner of my eye and saw she was moving her head imperceptibly, confused by everything that had happened.

I ran up to my room; I did not want my father to see me dressed like that. Then I went down to tell him goodnight and I ate no dinner. I went to bed right away.

Maybe some day, when I'm older, I will have developed a talent that right now I lack: the sense of continuity. I cannot even begin to imagine what grownups do the next day, after they've done something really terrible, after they're made fools of themselves or let themselves get completely carried away by some emotion, but I want to believe they behave consistently. It seems logical to me that some of them keep on with their foolishness and others hide it or try to erase it, depending on their personalities. I cannot do either of those things, the only thing I know how to do with my last spark of energy is die.

It's silly to talk about dying, since the idea of dying has never occurred to me and none of my foolishness has ever been important enough to warrant it. The reason I use that word is because I can find no other way to express how something ends at times like those, how something expires inside me. Suddenly my will is completely gone, and with it my memory and my understanding, as if the container that held them had been turned upside down and not a single drop was left.

The very fact that I reflect on this may be a sign that time is passing, but even so I'm afraid these eclipses will keep plaguing me forever; I'm afraid I will never face the consequences of my things until a hundred years after they happen. Then no one will remember them any longer and it will be absolutely impossible to do anything about them, since I will have lived through them with a stupidity that seems like blind egoism.

Can this be what people call innocence? How disgusting! I will never get tired of saying how disgusting I find this disease they call childhood. You fight to break out of it as if it were a nightmare, but you are like a sleepwalker; you make a few motions and then fall into a stupor again.

Today, now that I'm far away from what happened, I can call to mind how upsetting those moments were and relive their smallest details, because I myself was the person who took part in them, the person I am now. The day after, though, who was I the day after? I can only remember it the way you remember something that belongs to someone else, as if I had watched from a window and seen myself leave my house carrying my satchel of books under my arm. I was no more than a walking corpse. I have to go back to that idea of death. More than a corpse, though, I was an automaton — something that had never lived, because after a person dies the cadaver is left, with its natural alterations, and there are ruins left after an earthquake, but there is not even a trace left after that kind of death. Forgetfulness replaces life, the air you breathe, and time itself. The day of the celebration I was fifteen or twenty, the day after I was five or six.

There is something even more painful: adults regard these spills as something completely natural, the same way they find it natural for a two-year-old to take a tumble every now and then. They do not scold you for anything; they just toe the line themselves, which is their way of showing that they attach no importance whatsoever to anything that went on earlier.

Could anyone believe that after what happened we started to slide again toward a situation exactly like the one from a month before?

Some of the things Luisa and I talked about were even more secret than when we were planning the celebration. With don Daniel it was a question of gradually growing close again, in direct proportion to the way we each forgot what had happened. Because from the beginning mine was a forgetting to the death. His, though, and now I can see this clearly, was at first only a watchfulness, and it continued to lie low until the devastation left in me, the desert, immeasurable like my smallness, became apparent.

Then he was cordial again, he was generous again with his straightforward explanations, the ones that gave me the pleasure of understanding, that let me believe I was exercising my intelligence; and I accepted those explanations as if I still had faith in myself, as if I had not found out once and for all that he structured them that way deliberately.

How much did I have to forget before I could go back to

spending afternoons dipping my pen in the big hemispheric inkwell and gazing at violet ink through thick glass, without doing anything else, without another thought, savoring the silence in the study, which I found comfortable and pleasant, because not only was it inhabited by the objects on the desk, it was also enlivened by the books behind me on the shelves? From that silence I did not even think about the silence left outside. It must have been so arid, and above all so invincible, so limitless that Luisa would not struggle to break it; I am sure that her lack of intervention was voluntary. Maybe her anxiety conjured demonic forces, because the fact is they answered her cry for help. The way they answered proves they were demonic, because they answered like buzzards responding to the cries of someone who has fallen into a ditch.

It happened precisely in that hallway with the heavenly light, where the floor was always red and shiny. They rubbed wax into the ocher until it was like a mirror; I had thought many times that someone was bound to fall there.

One afternoon when I arrived, I found Luisa lying on the bed with don Daniel nearby; they had sent for him, and the maids were putting cloths with arnica on her knee. I was never able to find out how it happened.

You could tell from her expression that she was suffering horribly. There was no trace now of her usual serenity, that impassive grandeur, which did not seem at all insensitive or cold, which made her features look firm and ill defined, or distant, rather, at the same time, since none of the contractions that commonly alter people's faces ever registered on hers. I would say not that her serenity had been erased but that it had broken in fifty pieces.

Considering that the pain was localized there in her knee and had not spread anywhere else, and that it had been caused by a blow, and a blow caused by nothing more than a false step, the violence of Luisa's screaming and twitching was disproportionate, as if she were taking advantage of a long awaited opportunity. She complained with her voice, her hands, her eyes, as if to say: 'Why not? Now I can complain without feeling the least bit ashamed; anyone would complain about this.' But the way she complained made her seem to be complaining about something else.

I was almost afraid to get close to her, because I did not think she would recognize me, but I overcame that moment of horror, went over to her, and took one of her hands in mine. In fact her hand did not recognize me; it could not keep still between my hands because it was controlled by a feverishness that stiffened it and by a determination apparently bent on showing how ugly and embarrassing suffering can be.

The doctor finally came. He bandaged her leg and gave her a sedative. When she lay down on the pillow her features regained a little of their serenity, but in one hand she still held the handkerchief she had wadded into a ball; it was moist from being bitten and she was squeezing it hard.

I went home late, although there was nothing I could do for her, and first thing the next morning I went back to see how she was, but they had gone to Valladolid. She had spent the night in great pain, and as soon as it was daylight they had telephoned for a car to take her for X-rays.

I walked down to the highway automatically and leaned on the edge of the bridge, watching the road. It was absurd to wait for them so soon, since they had not been gone for even two hours, but until they came back I could not do anything else.

I walked around for a while and spent some time amusing the children; they seemed bewildered but did not make a fuss. I went home to explain what had happened, and my aunt was sorry, not that such an unfortunate thing had happened but that something had happened.

I went back to the bridge; on the water there were a few leaves that had just fallen from the poplars. I don't know why but it irritated me that there were so many of those leaves, as if in each one of them I expected to see something come that never came. I watched them approach from far away, seeing them draw closer and closer until they disappeared beneath my feet, through the arches of the bridge, and they kept me from thinking; I could not stop looking at them. Another and another, and in the distance, way in the depth of the valley where they came from, God knows what: the suspicion of some horrible scene, with screams and desperate gestures.

It took me a long time to make up my mind to think about what had happened, which is why I kept my eyes on the dry leaves. Each time my imagination would lead me to reflect on the scene from the day before, I would draw back and grasp at whatever might be passing by. Nevertheless, the moment came when I found myself reliving everything I had seen.

In the same way that one afternoon two phrases that passed between them caused me to imagine all their possible dialogues, after I had seen Luisa express her pain — or rather her anger or impatience with pain — I could not help but compare her with the flashes of gloom or melancholy I had discovered sometimes in don Daniel.

That kind of discord was very, very difficult to explain. Everything about Luisa was so harmonious, and both her manners and her words, even though there were usually few words, seemed so resolute; but suddenly she revealed her own weakness. I had glimpsed that on other occasions, but now what she revealed was that her beauty or, rather, her grandeur did not increase at those moments you could call critical. On the other hand, don Daniel was a hundred times more admirable when one of those sad looks crossed his face. All I had ever seen was something like the shadow of a thought that, at times, changed his features, and I had always been sorry he did not dwell on such thoughts, because it seemed to me that their realm was probably his true kingdom. Smiling or laughing out loud were things he did no differently from everyone else. Sometimes you could see ridicule in his smile; at other times there was intelligence, cruelty, or even happiness. That was seldom, and it never involved him alone. It might happen if he was participating in something that also involved other people, if he saw something pretty, an object or a beautiful animal.

On the other hand, when something painful or terrible crossed his mind, then he was unique. There was a sadness that came from his eyes, altered the light of his surroundings, and spread through them. Nothing on earth seemed immune to that sadness. It was like one of those gusts of flame that escape sometimes from an oven and let us glimpse for an instant the force trapped inside.

I waited for them from eight in the morning until six in the late afternoon. I did everything it's possible to do on one trip after another between their house and mine, and every little while I went back to the bridge; I could concentrate on these thoughts there, which made me feel I was with Luisa and don Daniel. That theme of pain was what seemed to let me get closest to them. In the uncertainty of waiting, hour after hour, there were moments when it seemed they would never come back.

Finally the car appeared in the distance. Don Daniel was sitting beside the driver, and Luisa was in the back with her legs stretched out on the seat. I got in and sat on the floor; that way between there and the house she could tell me what had happened.

She had recovered some of her serenity. There was a small fracture in her knee, but the doctors who examined her had said it was nothing serious; once it was healed it would not cause her any trouble. The only thing was she had six weeks in bed to look forward to because she had to stay off her feet entirely.

Getting her out of the car was really difficult. She could support herself on the left leg, but the other one was not to be moved or touched in any way. We all worked together and finally got her out of there. Then don Daniel picked her up as if she were a feather and carried her to the second floor in a minute. Before he put her in bed, Luisa told him:

'Wait a bit, it's better for them to slide the bed out from the wall so I can lower myself on my left side; that will make it easier for me to move.'

He started to argue with her that it made no difference, but Luisa added, 'That's the way I prefer it.'

The two maids moved the bed, leaving it about a yard away from the wall.

Don Daniel carried Luisa over to the corner so he could put her in bed, but she was still not ready.

'Pillows,' she said. 'Give me a lot of pillows.'

I had been observing throughout the whole operation, but how can I say that I observed what happened? If I had observed it, who would believe me? Can I consider my observation so extraordinary, or my talents so exceptional that they will infallibly surpass those of other human beings? No, I observed nothing: I was transported — if by chance I do have some exceptional gift, that's the only one — I was joined with Luisa, I identified with her at that moment. I went all through her soul and her five senses, the way we go through a beloved house, going over everything thoroughly. I saw everything that was in her thoughts, I sensed what her hands felt, I felt the feeling etched in her voice.

It was not hard for don Daniel to keep holding her; she had one arm wrapped around his neck and with the other hand she gave the impression of grabbing onto his opposite shoulder, but she did not grab onto anything, because it was unnecessary. All she did was run her hands lightly over his shoulders, as if she felt unsteady, as if she were trying to get a better grip, but she was not, she was doing something permissible that afternoon, which is why she was trying to draw things out with a kind of anxious look in her eyes and with an insistence that every last detail be arranged perfectly — something made possible by that briefest of circumstances — that let her touch the cloth on his suit, squeeze him slightly between her arm and her chest, then harder as she felt him lean over the bed, and detach herself slowly, as if it were very dangerous to let her head fall on the pillows at last.

Who could deny that I felt everything that was happening inside Luisa, as if I myself were inside her? The thousand questions I had wondered about at other times, including the things I could not understand and hoped she would tell me when I was older: suddenly it was all clear. In one moment I knew as much about her as she herself, and this time no selfish hesitation encumbered my emotion. What I lived in that moment was not some scheme devised by my own more or less provocative self-interest. No, I lived in her and exclusively for her, her life, her most intimate secrets, and I can swear that with her, from the depths of her being, I felt the thirstiness in the palms of her hands as they seemed to drink in the cloth of his suit.

The children wanted to get up on the bed so they could kiss their mother; I would not let them, I pulled them from the bed, saying they might hurt her a lot. I tried to protect her from all contact, to keep any noise away from her. I tried to keep my distance from her as well, to forget the moments before, and I went to the kitchen with the children; I stayed there with them for a while until it was time to put them to bed.

The next day there was a lot of activity in Luisa's room. In the morning, an assistant came from Valladolid to help the doctor put the cast on her leg, and in the afternoon the visits began. This went on for several days; all the ladies from Simancas put in an appearance there.

I would spend the whole day with her; of course I did no studying.

One afternoon when I went down from her room, I saw don Daniel in the study.

I went in resolutely. It was impossible to tell what kind of mood he was in from my first glance, but I started to talk about Luisa right away, before he could get his guard up. I asked him if it was true that the doctors had said the accident was not serious, and he answered without holding back any details. He drew the head of the bone on a piece of paper, exactly like he had seen it on the X-rays, and he showed me where they had discovered the fracture; it was nothing more than something like a splinter that was not completely detached. He assured me that it should knit perfectly and that she would experience absolutely no discomfort when she walked.

It was the first time the conversation there, in that room, was about what went on in the other rooms, but I had determined there would not be silence about the topic and there was not. Don Daniel agreed to talk, but not out of either weakness or duty: he liked my decision and responded magnanimously.

The whole first week nothing unusual happened. On the afternoon of the eighth day two ladies came. One of them was wicked; you could tell just by looking at her; the other was dumb, totally stupid, and there was nothing special during the first part of the conversation. As always, Luisa was completely removed from all squabbling about household concerns and neighborhood gossip.

Suddenly the wicked one started to say that Luisa must be very happy to have two such beautiful little boys. Luisa nodded her head yes, smiling a little; the lady went on to say they looked

139

so much like their father it was a shame she did not also have a daughter who looked like her. Luisa glanced away from that lady and let her gaze rest on the gaze of the other one, who had very peaceful eyes. The assurance given off by those eyes inspired her.

'Yes,' she answered, 'it would be very nice to have a daughter who resembled her father, because the boys are too much like me.'

'But doña Luisa,' the stupid lady answered, 'you're almost blond. How can you say they resemble you?'

'I'm referring to their character,' Luisa said.

'Sometimes children get their physical appearance from their father,' said the wicked lady, 'and their character from their mother; sometimes it's the reverse. The thing is, parents are never satisfied.'

It seemed as though she was about to shut up, but she decided to continue:

'Which shows that you're a model wife, because you find the best thing about your husband to be his character.'

Luisa smiled and raised one hand to her forehead; she did not bother to point out that what she had meant was something entirely different.

One more secret! I thought. Her face apparently remained as serene as always. Then I saw, though, a succession of small grimaces becoming engraved there; each one was different, and I realized that they left a trail of her thoughts, although I could not have detected them before. What I felt reminded me of those times in the pine grove when I started to look for pine cones in the grass and at first I could not make out anything in the sameness of so much green; after I spotted the first one, though, pine cones would immediately start turning up everywhere, because then I could see the chiaroscuro that gave them away.

I was afraid she would notice that I was looking at her differently, so I tried for a stare that would make me seem puzzled or tired; that way I could keep studying the area newly open to my investigation.

Don Daniel appeared in her room several times every afternoon, but just briefly; he would say a few words and then leave. One afternoon he alluded to the way I'd given up my studies; it was said as a joke and a completely harmless joke. He said it was odd that I would harbor such a lazy streak. Then he added that the reason he found it odd was that no one would suspect such a thing; I would get all wrapped up in my studies, but as soon as the first opportunity came along I would lapse enthusiastically into idleness.

While don Daniel was talking about this, I was fixing Luisa a cup of coffee, so I did not look at him; I sort of pretended I could not hear, because he was so right it was making me laugh deep down inside. When I heard him continue, though, as if he were apologizing for what he had said, as if he wanted to rationalize it with all kinds of explanations, like 'it's only a comment, it's a psychological observation,' I realized that his apologies were not meant for me, and I looked at Luisa.

She was lying against the pillows, leaning a little to her left, with her forehead resting on one hand and the other arm stretched out alongside her body. Who could have guessed what passions were stirring in her soul? No one but me. I saw that even though her eyes were half closed they were fixed in an oblique gaze and that her lashes pointed in the same direction as her eyes because her eyelid was a little swollen at the point where it touched the cornea; this made her lashes look like spears. That gaze was threatening, but in the way a person threatens both angrily and anxiously at the same time. What it said precisely was: 'You want to take away the only thing I have.'

In order to draw her out of those thoughts I made her drink

the coffee and plied her with questions about whether it was too strong or too weak, too sweet or too bitter, if it was enough or if she wanted more. Meanwhile, don Daniel disappeared; he vanished from the room, and we did not even hear his footsteps on the stairs. A long while later, when it seemed impossible even to remember the incident from before, and without mentioning it, without giving any indication or referring to it, as if in fact the flow of conversation had not been interrupted by so much as a comma, Luisa said:

'The truth is you've lost almost the entire month of September, and it seems impossible that you'll be able to prepare for an exam between now and June.'

I just shrugged my shoulders, not as if to say that I didn't care but that we would see.

'Go study now, don't lose even one more afternoon,' she told me the next day in a perfectly natural tone.

After hesitating a little, I went, because I thought that if I waited until don Daniel came back it would take more of an effort.

A short while later he appeared at the door, said 'hello' to me, walked around the room a bit, finally sat down, and opened a book. No allusion to my sloth, no irony. Also, the studying was more serious and more intense than ever. It was rigorous in a different way, though: not forced but efficient and clear, so things moved along as if they were on wheels.

Luisa managed to do something unbelievable: she managed to surpass a serenity I thought unsurpassable. Could she have felt that I was attacking her, that I had found the breach? I don't know, the thing is when I arrived in the mornings everything around her would be already straightened up: her hair would be combed, she would be all dressed, and her back would be resting against the pillows as if she had set up headquarters there for devoting herself to trivial activities.

One day after we were already into the second week, I found her bed completely covered with things: boxes of necklaces she was arranging and several books. Next to her she had an English novel and a dictionary; I could see the edge of a small blue pamphlet sticking out from the pages of the dictionary.

Luisa picked up the dictionary. 'Last night I started to read this book and I found something inside,' she said. 'I bet you don't know what it is.'

She pointed to the little blue edge protruding from the dictionary. Since I shook my head no, she went on:

'It's something I put in the dictionary the first day you came to this house. I meant to give it to you, and then I forgot.'

She pulled it out.

'See?' she said, 'It's the theory for the first year of solfeggio. That's why you came. Remember?'

The evocation was overpowering, and I felt myself carried back to that day with indescribable longing.

'Of course,' she continued, 'last year I was in no position to take on something like that; and books were better for you, since you're already too old to start solfeggio with any thought of playing seriously. Besides, you don't have the temperament for spending hours every day sitting at the piano; even so, it's a shame.'

'Yes, it's a shame.'

The pamphlet was in my hands then, and I was leafing through it.

'What would be necessary,' Luisa went on, 'when the time came, would be to find your voice placement, because you could learn to sing, and sing very well.'

'I don't know,' I said, 'I can't manage the high notes; as soon as I try, my voice fails me.'

'Because you're a contralto and you always pitch things too high; it's a question of teaching you. Since you should not push your voice too soon, it would have been better if you had mastered solfeggio for when your voice has matured.'

That afternoon I took great care not to let my satchel fall to the floor because the little blue notebook was inside my books. And the next morning, sitting on Luisa's bed, I ventured on that new discipline, in a way very different from the droning in choir practice some months before.

I learned to read music right away, and in the first lesson I was familiar with all the signs: it was very, very easy for me. Before and after the lesson, we talked about what I could learn to sing. Luisa listed all the operas for me where the contralto had an important role; she told me the plots and in a low voice she sang to me some passages she knew in Italian, French, and even German. She knew more *romanzas* than I could count, tunes from every country; there was a true musical geography in her head, but she never sang because she didn't have much of a voice and also because singing did not fit her personality.

Perhaps that was exactly why she wanted me to sing. She felt very impatient to be able to get up and get things under way. In just two or three more weeks, we would be able to go to Valladolid and look for pieces that were appropriate for my voice; if they were not, she would transpose them.

What I found most admirable was watching her write music. She would hum things she had half forgotten, jotting them down with her pencil on pieces of ruled paper that were with the solfeggio exercises. I had never seen music being written that way. The musical signs, so stiff and severe on the printed page, were reduced to light scribbles there, to frills and little tails, which always slanted because Luisa's hand moved so fast, giving them the smooth obliqueness of English Roundhand.

We had been having lessons for three or four days, just in the mornings; in the afternoon all that was banished. I would go up to see Luisa when I arrived, but I only stayed with her for a

144

minute; when I closed the door to her room, everything stayed inside there and I would start to work furiously in the study with great determination.

I was sure there was not a clue that might have led don Daniel to find out I was wasting my time. I would pick up all the exercises and papers before he came back at midday and Luisa was as careful as I not to mention it. Nevertheless, I don't know if it was all of a sudden, or little by little; I don't know if it was consciously or just as a hunch, but the fact is once again don Daniel started to exude distrust, irony, and bitterness.

Concerning this, I am faced with a difficulty that I'm not sure I can overcome. I wish I could record here a doubt that struck me at the time of those events and which I have still not been able to clear up. Not only have I been unable to clear it up; I have not even been able to think about it. It's been hovering around me, threatening me, and I have not had the courage to confront it.

In the first place, there is no reason the same things that happen to me would not happen to everyone else. Just because I have never noticed them happening to other people does not mean they don't, but it does lead me to think that since I don't find out what happens to other people, other people won't find out what happened to me.

It seems like a fair deduction, but no, it isn't: it has to be stated differently.

I think there are times when I can get into other people's souls, merge and identify with other people. The only thing that would prove this is not just something I imagine would be some perception of it on the part of other people. Since they don't show any signs of that, the logical conclusion is that they are not aware of it. It could also be, though, that when I think I'm exercising my will, all I'm doing is obeying a summons and that others are left just like me, not knowing if anyone answered them, because no one is capable of confessing this kind of secret.

Only saints, those souls who have spent their whole lives in contemplation, are sure of receiving a response, and perhaps this not knowing, this resistance to confession among human beings, proves it's a grave sin to play around with these things. It is so grave you cannot even explain it in confession at church. A thousand times I have resolved to make a full confession of all these escapades my soul has gotten involved in, but that's been late at night, when my anxiety was so great I felt I was really foundering in it.

In the morning I either remembered nothing or I remembered something so cold and so insignificant, that my confessor would say, 'Bah, that's nothing, don't pay any attention to those fantasies!'

Why am I confessing them now? Because it's after one o'clock, because sometimes I get up from the desk, go over to the window, and peer out through the double panes at a night that looks frozen. I leaf through what I have written and see how flat and monotonous it is; I search, scour the depths of the anguish invading me and I find this and write it, because what's happening to me is that I'm afraid of going forward. I can still say something more about those secret, unclear events; I can still remember infinite details, before moving on to something else.

I have already said there were no clues that might have given away my diversions. There were no material clues, but in an automatic, hopeless way the same phenomenon as always was recurring. I was studying, multiplying my efforts a hundred times, and I was having good results. But then, instead of becoming focused or being consumed by my studies, the usual host of lateral ideas kept buzzing around me, and the predominant ideas were the ones stemming from recent experiences, the ones that had become real and been illuminated by emotions that were still close.

Were those ideas really powerful enough to engulf a person? Was it a question of creating repercussions that in effect transmitted the very nature of the ideas themselves, or did those ideas coincidentally meet up with other ideas that were different but nevertheless congenial?

All I could tell for sure was that the times we were sitting at the desk, don Daniel talking and me listening, all of a sudden he would look away from me abruptly. Not how you look away from another person because you feel intimidated. No, he could never feel that way: the direction of his gaze would change unexpectedly, as if he needed to throw light on an idea that had suddenly struck him, and he would stare into a dark corner, where terrible phantoms must have been emerging for him.

How can I put it? It, what was reflected on his face at those moments—as fleetingly as when the flickering of a candle makes the shadows waver, as if the visions in the corner cast on him the mournful dance of a black veil—was exactly what I had been wanting to provoke with my thoughts.

The subject discussed on the page of the book open in front of us could have been anything, geography or grammar; between one paragraph and the next, between question and answer, sometimes during a long, complicated sentence, my thoughts would become lodged in an obsession with pain.

A concrete pain, in some place or from some thing, understandably sad ideas? Nothing like that: all I did was invoke pain, like those characters in Northern tales who call out to fright in their flight through the woods.

If I were perverse, and in addition so stupid that I lacked even the intelligence to recognize my own stupidity, all this would prove degrading for me, but I sincerely believe this is not what's happening to me: I believe it's something different.

In the first place, I see now that it was not pain I was invoking but horror; something outside of the everyday, one of those feelings or situations they refer to as 'tests.' How could I have wanted to draw pain toward a being I adored and admired more than anything else? What was happening was that only a limited part of his personality came into play in his day-to-day contact with me, and I saw such magnificence in him that I found it hard to resign myself to sharing in only one small part.

Then, Luisa's accident, my reflections that day when the long wait on the bridge had loaded my head with distressing thoughts and painful reflections, is what had led me to come up with something like a formula for my experiments with him.

Be that as it may, the only thing for sure is that I was thinking, at the same time I seemed to be listening, about what I called the painful or terrible ideas, that I yearned with all my might for a chance to study one of his expressions or catch one of his stormy looks when he was not expecting it, and that what made those expressions and looks appear was the intensity of my determination.

From them came all of don Daniel's irritation and bitterness. One afternoon he cut off the lesson brusquely, saying he had to go to out somewhere. The next day, before we started the lesson, his questions were already venomous.

'Have you studied everything?'

'Everything.'

'And you know it?'

'Of course.'

'Such a talent, such a talent! Let's continue.'

He tossed me that little phrase from an old *zarzuela*, which goes with a certain catchy tune from the operetta. He had said it to me before and had said it at such times that to repeat it now was to consider war declared. I knew it was followed by his enigmatic explanations and questions a person could never suspect.

He saw that his threat had put me so much on my guard that maybe he decided to disappoint me, and he was no more than moderately cruel.

I don't know if I was completely discouraged when I went to Luisa's room the next morning or if I saw her in that state and ended up falling into it myself.

Luisa had been bearing her illness with heroic patience. After the day she fell, she had never complained again, as if she had decided to deprive suffering of all importance by refusing to treat it as anything unusual. That morning, though, we had hardly gone through one lesson when she said she was not feeling well because she had spent a really bad night. She had the sensation that the leg in the cast had fallen asleep. In addition, the doctor had been there early and told her she would not be able to get up at the end of six weeks and that she would probably need a couple of weeks more.

The whole morning it was as if we had both been crushed, as if we felt that having dreams or making plans did us no good, that everything we wanted was liable to being delayed, interrupted, or wrecked. We seemed to be waiting for some solution to present itself suddenly, but the only thing that came was noon and, of course, don Daniel returning from the Archive.

I heard his footsteps as soon as he came in the front door, but I was incapable of gathering up the exercises.

The other days, I had done it naturally, as if to say the lesson was over; to do it at that moment would have been to show Luisa I was hiding the lessons — something she knew full well — and I did not do it. I saw her wait expectantly for a bit, and then together we faced the inquisitorial gaze that took note of everything in a minute but remained totally impassive, as if it had seen nothing.

I went back first thing in the afternoon, closed myself up downstairs, and opened my books. Time passed, time like a large glob, and I thought don Daniel was not going to come, but I heard a clock striking five and soon he appeared as usual.

After his customary 'hello' he went toward the bookshelf. I heard him rustling books, walking from one side to the other; I was strong enough to keep from turning my head.

'The history book we were looking for the other day finally turned up,' he said suddenly. 'You can take it home and read it; that is, if you have the energy left after all your many activities.'

The firing has started, I said to myself. Not to answer is to answer, to show that he's hit his mark and that I'm willing to keep on getting shot. Why not change my attitude, why not answer so sincerely it will make his whole game of innuendos impossible? I turned a little and looked at him.

'Don't think I've started to study music seriously,' I started out by saying. 'I'm only getting a bit of training, because right now' (I was about to say, 'Luisa says,' but I stopped myself) 'it's still too soon to find my voice placement. Later, when I'm older, I'd like to sing well.'

I succeeded in disarming him, but for less than a minute. When I started to speak, the innocence and frankness of my tone impressed him, and almost inadvertently, he adopted a similar attitude as he started to listen to me. Once he realized what my words meant, though, he raised his eyebrows with affected amazement, letting out an 'ah!' that went on forever, while he gathered irony.

'So you're going to devote yourself to *bel canto?*' he said.

I did not give up.

'I wouldn't think of singing professionally,' I answered in the same tone as before, 'but the truth is I'd like to sing with some evidence of training.'

'Perfect, perfect,' he exclaimed, slapping the palm of his hand against the spine of the book he was holding. 'You couldn't have thought of anything more perfect or more appropriate. Why did it take me so long to see you were an artist?'

He came toward the desk, put down the book, and looked at me like . . . I could not begin to say like what . . .

'That's exactly what you are,' he continued, 'an artist from head to toe: a real artist. I think you're capable of taking Rome by storm.'

He said nothing more; there was a short, frightening silence, and he left abruptly. As he left, though, I could hear something like teeth grinding, or a small laugh, or a slight cough. There was a creaking sound in his throat or his mouth, as inhuman as the creaking of a closet door. One of those noises that cause terror precisely because we don't know whether or not they're made by a person.

When they tell us about hell, we always imagine a cavern, a pit deep in the dark, impassable bowels of the earth; on the other hand, we always conceive of heaven as a vague, boundless immensity. Well, at that moment, I plunged into an immensity of misery dark as hell and boundless as heaven. But there is no point trying to explain what it was like, better to explain that I suddenly sensed that everything was about to stop existing.

I fell on the sofa, face down, and buried my head in the cushions. I wanted to keep my sobs from being heard outside the room, and their thundering was driving me crazy.

I don't know how long I spent that way nor why I suddenly lifted my head. Don Daniel was leaning against the doorjamb: my tears ended sharply.

The cruelty, the inhumanity, and the irony were completely gone from his face; all that was left was the other thing, horrible and indefinable.

He walked in and closed the door behind him. Even though his lips were half open he was clenching his teeth, so I don't see how he could have said anything, but he did.

'I'll kill you,' he told me. 'I'll kill you.'

What I have left to say now is something entirely different. If I could keep filling pages with forgotten details of images or thoughts, that would mean life continued; but no, it does not continue.

I'm afraid that telling about this other thing is more than I have strength for; I'm afraid that it's too hard for me, that I won't be able to make it perfectly clear what impossible things are like, or to show how a person can live in such an environment, knowing those things are about to explode at any minute, when everything will be shattered.

No; no, I don't need a different method. It's stupid to try to describe a high fever; it's enough to tell how high it got. It's enough to list the things that happened, one after the other, passing over them quickly until you get to the end, and that's all.

Nothing happened the next day; there's nothing to say about me. I did not go to see Luisa in the morning, I did not go and that's all: without further explanation. I went in the afternoon, but I did not go upstairs, the same way. The next day, however — since the next day came — I did not go to see Luisa either, but I did think about not having gone and I thought that going, if I ended up going the next day, was something that could only be compared to walking beside the river, but instead of following along the shore, turning and continuing to the bottom. That is technically possible, but who could do it?

I did not go to see Luisa the next day either. In the morning I did not go and in the afternoon I did not go upstairs, but of course I was obsessed with seeing her and convinced that seeing her was impossible; those feelings took up the whole day, the day and the night, and they destroyed everything.

They even destroyed my faculty of understanding the simplest things. Ever since I was very little, I had always had a natural talent for being able to overhear a word in passing and figure out whatever intrigue or complicated scheme people might have up their sleeves. Well, on the fourth day in the hall of my own house I heard those filthy remarks the housekeeper went around making and I did not understand.

What would I have done if I had understood? What could I have saved? Nothing, since by then it was too late.

Suddenly, I remember something now that strikes me as too trivial to mention, because it breaks into what I intended to be a narration of nothing but the bare facts. But it proves, even though it resembles a fantasy, a diversion like the ones from before, that as I listened to the housekeeper I already understood how useless understanding is.

That whole fourth day I was bothered by one fixed idea. Suddenly I asked myself: when you're out in the country, why is it you never see dead birds, dead rabbits, rats, or other small animals? I found the answer right away: those animals live only as long as they have the energy to run from their enemies; after a certain time they fall, succumb, because they're surrounded by danger on all sides.

I thought about the birds and the rabbits. It seemed to me I was taking refuge in that idea so I would not have to think about anything else, so I could get the other ideas out of my head. But I was not; I was thinking about that so I could understand how at a certain moment it's too late to run away.

The fifth day I did not go to see Luisa in the morning, I did not go up in the afternoon, and the study door closed again.

Without warning, the latch jerked violently and for a moment the whole door was shaken vigorously. I was sitting in front of the desk. Don Daniel opened; it was my father.

I could hear don Daniel saying a word I did not understand; I only sensed that his tone was courteous and serene.

My father came in without saying anything, closed the door, and leaned his back against it.

'Above all,' he said, 'don't raise your voice.'

'I have no reason to,' don Daniel answered.

I want to transcribe here letter by letter all the words heard inside there, but how can I transcribe the silences?

It was impossible to tell which of the two was in control of the situation. My father was there, not moving, filled with a resolution that could not be shaken by anyone or anything. And don Daniel, steady thanks to a serenity that seemed capable of withstanding everything. All of a sudden, his gaze swerved a little and he moved slightly, which made me afraid he lacked strength; he thought about me being there; he wanted to tell my father that he should make me leave, but he saw that my father would not listen to him so he said nothing; he recovered his serenity.

My father began to say such strange things. For a moment at first it seemed as though he might not be in his right mind, but he was; it was just that he started to speak as though someone had interrupted him and he was picking up where he had left off.

'When a person has done something once in his life, he does not repeat it,' he said. 'No, there's no need to worry that he'll repeat it.'

Don Daniel listened to him without saying anything; my father continued.

'I could perfectly well do what you're thinking, but I'm not going to do it. I know what that involves: I did it once ten years ago and I wound up here, alone' — he rapped on the floor with his crutch — 'here, alone, but standing. Do you think I'm about to test my luck again?'

Don Daniel did not answer.

'This time it's your turn. I'm going to permit myself that

satisfaction. It's very easy. From my house, without budging, I'm going to watch you leave here with your whole entourage: with dishonor, with scandal, with a well-aimed blow, one of those blows that fouls up a man for the rest of his life. It's very easy, all I have to do is request your dismissal for . . .'

I think there was one more word, but I could not hear it. Without losing its restrained tone, don Daniel's voice cut my father off so sharply it obliterated what he was saying.

'Make Leticia leave the room,' he exclaimed.

My father did not budge, did not even turn his head toward me.

'Don't interrupt me,' was all he said.

But don Daniel had interrupted him; he tried to start again and he continued relentlessly, but not as overwhelmingly as before.

'I even have the satisfaction of seeing you leave in good company. You don't have the option of going off to the Rif, you drag along three others, and they'll have as hard a time as you yourself.'

His words were as monstrous as one of those tortures that finally reduce the victim to shrieks and convulsions, but they seemed to spread a great peace over don Daniel's face. The way he moved his eyebrows suggested clearly that any attack was useless, and my father's rage dropped yet another notch.

My father kept on talking; I don't think I missed anything, I think I've been able to reconstruct all of it, because at that moment I was no more than a piece of rubbish, one of those plants yanked from the ground in winter and thrown in the ditch, where it stays all dead and frozen.

'I suppose you won't deny this.'

His tone was rather questioning, and he paused, leaving space for a response.

Don Daniel took his time, and he did not respond in agreement; he began to speak, as if he were initiating the conversation:

'I don't know how you set it up the other time, but I imagine the other man was at least permitted to hold a weapon.'

'Of course he had a weapon,' my father said.

'Then, give me the right to use a few words.'

My father shrugged his shoulders, conceding indifferently. Don Daniel thought a little while longer and finally he spoke:

'Your attitude is understandable; I can see why the plan you've outlined is the only one that will satisfy you. What I'm going to say is in no way either a warning or a recommendation; in short, it's the following: what you propose cannot happen.'

My father started to get angry.

'I've never seen such cynicism,' he almost shouted.

'You know perfectly well,' don Daniel replied, 'that what you are seeing is not cynicism,' and he continued because my father could not answer quickly. 'If, when you leave here, you reflect for even half an hour, you will see that what you have just laid out is not feasible. It's all planned with great refinement, and you've spared nothing so as to make it thoroughly monstrous, but you have not considered that something might make it impossible.'

My father was inwardly disconcerted, but he did not show it, and since he did not have an answer and could not figure out what enigma don Daniel was referring to, he decided to remain silent, letting it seem as though he were waiting for him to finish.

'After you go out this door,' don Daniel said, 'a little while later you'll understand.'

As he said this, he nodded toward the door, and my father detached himself from it, as if he were inadvertently obeying that nod. He started to move slowly and laboriously, trying to

156

balance himself with his crutches, as if he were about to leave, but don Daniel stopped him then with a gesture.

'I'd still like to tell you,' he began. 'Well, I don't need to, because time will prove this as well; I only want to say that I'm certain about it before anything can prove it. I'm referring to the importance in the future . . . There's a word that I don't even want to use; but if, after all, I refer to the moral future, I mean the way this unfolds in the future . . . About this point I know very well there is nothing to fear.'

That's when my father exclaimed, 'It's inconceivable! In all the days I have left I'll never be able to repeat it enough! It's inconceivable, it's inconceivable!'

'Think about what I've said,' don Daniel continued. 'The incident is so inordinate it won't fit in your plans, no matter how perfect they are. It has to resolve itself on its own. Think about this, colonel, think about it if only for half an hour.'

My father kept repeating the same word in a low voice, and now that he had moved away from the door, he took a few unsteady steps, as if he wanted to justify the confusion in his head with the clumsiness in his feet.

With an indescribable swiftness, as soon as he saw a small space free, don Daniel grabbed me by the arm almost at the shoulder—I thought my arm was going to come off my body—opened the door about a foot and a half and threw me out.

The momentum from his hand seemed to carry me home through the air: I did not feel the ground under my feet.

I went in through the door off the garden, but I did not walk through the kitchen; I walked up a little stairway that led to the balcony, and from the balcony to the upstairs hallway. I went to my room and locked the door from inside.

I listened for a while; the maid had seen me from the back of the kitchen, but no one followed me upstairs. There was a silence as if the house were empty. I looked out from the windows on the balcony; none of the lights were lit yet, but in spite of the darkness I could make out my father turning the corner. Each time he took a step he would try to cover a large distance, but then he would totter before taking another step, so he was making difficult progress. I stared at him, trying to guess his mood from the way he was moving toward me. The sidewalk was enveloped in shadows, but a transparent sky above the houses caught my gaze and held it. At the center of that stillness I sensed something like a bubble bursting. The bang was small, distant, and so short that a person wondered if something so devoid of time could be real. For a moment I ran my eyes over the entire area, looking for a trace, a confirmation: everything was just as still as before, except that my father tottered even more on the sidewalk below. He turned and retraced a few steps; then he stopped to listen, took another step toward the house, and stopped again. Suddenly he started to walk wildly, as if with total disregard for all his infirmities, riding roughshod over himself. He went in at the front, and the whole house shook when he slammed the door to his room.

Silence returned, and outside the same total stillness. Suddenly a man ran by to the right, and a minute later another man went running after him; they met up when they were well in the distance and began to pat each other on the back; they were just two boys playing. All the street lights went on and at first it was harder for me to see. The street seemed much darker, with a shiny point on each corner.

A car passed that seemed to be from out of town and it stopped after turning the corner beside our house, next to the wall of our garden, but I heard nothing else. I kept looking out the window, studying the figures of hurried women passing beneath the street lights too fast for me to find out from their expressions if they were going somewhere, if they knew something.

158

I began to hear voices at the front door, several voices; they were all murmuring and they all jumbled together. The only thing I could make out was that in the midst of all those people my Aunt Aurelia was crying, but she was not whimpering the way she did other times: she was choking, really crying. That was all I needed to know, but I could not cry; I still waited for the miracle.

The door to my father's room closed again loudly, and again there was silence in the doorway; I sat down on the edge of the bed.

Why did I say nothing? From cowardice? From indifference? No, only because I knew that what I would have wanted to do was not possible. There was nowhere I could have gotten to; if I had gone out the door, one of the servants from my house or a man in the street could have crushed me the way you step on a rat.

I stayed there in silence in the half dark room.

The door to my father's room closed again, softly this time. A few footsteps went past the front door and started up the stairs; a few footsteps of a man walking quickly and agilely upstairs. In that minute I thought and lived a hallucination as strong as a mirage must be in the desert: it was hope, pounding in my heart as the footsteps approached my door. Finally, a few raps of the knuckles and a voice calling me by name. I recognized the voice immediately: it was my Uncle Alberto.

'Open up right now,' he demanded, 'open this minute.'

I opened. He entered and started to look all around.

'Hurry up, let's go,' was all he said. 'You're coming with me.'

He pounced on a sewing basket in one corner and emptied it onto the bed; then he opened a drawer and tossed a handful of things into the basket.

'Let's go,' he said, talking all the while. 'Don't waste time; put on a coat.'

He took a few dresses from the closet and threw them over his arm. He shook me a little because I was not reacting. Almost dragging me to the door, he told me with an affectionate gesture:

'Silence, for now; you and I will talk later.'

We went down the little stairway from the balcony, because my uncle had left the car at the back door. We did not meet anyone on the way; we got into the car and set out for Valladolid.

I could consider the story finished. It's March now. Five months have passed and my life during that time has been as foreign to me as the life of any person in this city, whose language I barely know.

I remember that when I started this notebook I laid plans for acting in opposition to my surroundings: I've reneged on all of those plans. I've studied with Adriana and I've let myself go gliding over the snow the same as everyone else.

My Aunt Frida continues to think I'm a good girl; both she and her husband have made it something of their mission to convince me of that.

In Valladolid, the night I spent in the hotel, in the room next to my uncle's, where he had me hidden until it was time to catch the train so news of the incident would not spread to my grandmother's house, he was already trying to cheer me up with an argument along those lines. 'What happened is not your fault,' he repeated over and over. 'It was bound to happen; if it hadn't been for this, it would have been for something else. In the end, the only person responsible is your father because he should have put you in the right environment a long time ago,' etc.

I looked at him silently and wondered inside: What would happen if I told him right now that it makes me sick to listen to him? What would happen if I kicked him? He'd take me back to Simancas again, and no, I am not strong enough to walk slowly down to the bottom of the river.

At the same time I could see that he had the best of intentions, that he had done and would continue to do everything possible to save me, but the thing was I considered it degrading to let myself be saved, knowing that I did not deserve to be saved. I did let myself, though.

He thought he had comforted me and advised me to get some sleep so I would not be tired when we started the trip. As he was going to his room, he showed me his ticket, which he had purchased the day before.

'I had come from buying it just when Aurelia phoned me to ask for help.'

And he added, with the smugness of people who are sure they know how to fix things:

'Come on, if it hadn't been for me, you would have been lost, dear.'

It's wonderful to cry in a room where the light from the hall enters through the transom over the door and you can be looking at one of those coat stands with twisted hooks made in Vitoria, or in the berth of a train too, close to the ceiling, near the little blue light, where you can smell the smoke that comes in when you go through the tunnels and feel the vibration rocking you as if the train were some powerful being carrying you in its arms as it runs along.

All this is wonderful, but it's repugnant that all this is offered to even the most despicable creature. Although I don't know if finding it repugnant might be refusing to understand God's mercy.

Maybe I don't understand it? I don't know; I believe that if any gratitude exists in me, it exists only in the form of brute force. It's something irrational, something like health. When I feel the cold on my cheeks, when I run with Adriana through the snow or among the dark trees covering these hillsides, a certain goodness invades me, almost making me smile, and I'm enraptured by beautiful things.

Suddenly I'm remembering . . . no, that I will not write. I described all of my lofty sentiments until they finally led me to what happened, because that's why I did this: so it would be clear exactly what came of those sentiments. About the way things are now I don't want to say a word, I do not want my suffering to be moving; on the contrary, if I keep writing it's only because I do not want to skip over this web of grotesque details being woven around me, for my own good.

My aunt loves to show me off to her friends, along with her archaeological research on the Mediterranean. Several of them usually come to have tea with her, next to the fireplace; then they work on their *tricot*, and they all talk at once. When Adriana and I come in from the street and I take off my cape, they all admire my curls, which they say are black. There's one of them who always calls me 'Mignon,' and one day she said she would have to teach me some poetry that begins: 'Do you know the country where the orange tree blooms?'

At this, my aunt took the opportunity to explain the differences between Italy and Spain, and she also told them that I don't have any of the characteristics of people you find in the south, and that there are no orange trees in the region where I was born, although there is a wonderful castle filled with documents.

I left the room then, after telling the woman I have a very poor memory for poetry, and Adriana followed behind, delightedly admiring my ability to tell a lie like that.

When they all left, I went over to the fire and sat on the stone bench beside the hearth. Adriana was studying and I sat there a long time, eating the slices of bread left from tea. My uncle came home, and something he said to his wife made me pay attention in a hurry. The could not see me, because I was hidden by an enormous armchair that happened to be in front of me. They were talking about a letter from Spain and they went over to a lamp so they could read it. I don't know who the letter was from, probably one of my aunts. 'They've done the right thing,' my uncle said. 'Poor Aurelia couldn't take any more.'

The right thing they had done was leave the house in Simancas.

Then he began to explain to my aunt that *the other time* my father had also gone to Margarita Velayos's house in the country; he had stayed there a few months before he went to Africa, and who knows how long it will be now. Then they talked again about how the only good decision had been to give up the house. This was what reassured them. Now, with the three of us separated we were less dangerous; not a word about the rest of it. Not a remark, not even an allusion to the drama that had caused everything. But I knew very well what they were thinking: they were thinking that if it had not been for one reason it would have been for another.

Besides, my aunt made it very clear that to some extent she had foreseen it all. 'That's what I told you from the beginning,' she kept repeating. 'It couldn't be, it was crazy. That couldn't be, it couldn't be.'

They did not realize that what couldn't be was behind the armchair.

I don't know if it was anger or bitterness that brought tears to my eyes. It seemed then that as long as I lived, I would never again feel anything you could call love in any form.

Afterward, it occurred to me that what I called brute force might be the only certainty I had left. Then I started to yawn and to feel a tremendous desire for a good sound sleep. I had not stopped eating black bread even though I was crying.

I walked calmly out from the corner, and even though they

were shocked, they thought it was better to make nothing of it, better to assume I had not heard anything.

I said I was tired and that I wanted to go to bed; nobody objected.

When I got to my room I remembered that the next day was March 10. I looked at the branch of ivy climbing up the window frame and the amount it had grown was what I had calculated.

Translator's Afterword: 13 Glosses

CAROL MAIER

1. ROSA CHACEL was born in Valladolid, Spain, in 1898, a year that also brought the end of the Spanish Empire and the birth of poet Federico García Lorca. Like García Lorca and others born near the turn of the century (for example, Luis Buñuel, Salvador Dalí, Pedro Salinas, Luis Cernuda), as well as slightly older figures such as Juan Ramón Jiménez, Chacel would contribute to what she has referred to as Spain's 'Golden Decade' (*decáda de oro*) of the 1920s.

The best account of Chacel's childhood is *Desde el amanecer* (Since dawn), the autobiography of her first ten years.[1] As she describes them, both her parents had strong artistic and literary interests and talents. Her mother was a teacher and her father had studied at the Academia Militar. When Rosa was ten, the family moved to Madrid. She was frequently in poor health as a child, and this was responsible to a large extent for the fact that she had little formal schooling. Although she began to write when she was a young girl, Chacel's initial intention was to be a sculptor. She began to study art at the age of eight, and at seventeen she enrolled at the Escuela de Bellas Artes de San Fernando, in Madrid. While studying there, she met Timoteo Pérez Rubio, a painter, whom she married in 1921. Between 1922 and 1927 the couple lived in Rome, where Pérez Rubio had a grant to study at the Academia de España.

During the years in Rome, Chacel read voraciously and wrote her first novel, *Estación. Ida y vuelta* (Station. Round trip), whose protagonist she has defined as the philosophy of José Ortega y Gasset. She did not know Ortega personally before leaving Madrid, but she was strongly influenced by his work, in particular his vision of a more open, Europeanized Spain and his determination to redirect Spanish prose. On her return to Madrid, Chacel met Ortega and contributed to the *Revista de Occidente*, the magazine he had founded; it had already published the first chapter of her *Estación* while she was still in Rome. Her second novel, *Teresa*, a biography of Teresa Mancha, the mistress of Spanish Romantic poet José Espronceda, was written at Ortega's suggestion. Chacel began work on it in 1930, but the birth of her son, Carlos, in that year slowed her progress. The first chapter was published in the *Revista de Occidente*, but the novel was not finished until 1936 and not published in its entirety until 1941.

By that time, Chacel was no longer living in Spain, having left with Carlos soon after the outbreak of the Spanish Civil War. For several years, she lived in Europe (Paris, Greece, Switzerland) while Pérez Rubio remained in Spain as president of the Junta de Defensa del Tesoro Artístico Nacional. After the defeat of the Spanish Republic in 1939, Pérez Rubio joined his wife and son, and in 1940 the three of them sailed from Bordeaux for Rio de Janeiro. Until 1974, when she returned to Spain permanently, Chacel lived primarily in South America, much of the time in Rio but often in Buenos Aires as well, where she had friends and contributed regularly to the literary journal *Sur. Memorias de Leticia Valle*, her third novel but the first she calls her 'own' (written without Ortega's direct influence), was published in Buenos Aires in 1945. Between 1959 and 1961 she lived in New York as the recipient of a Guggenheim Fellowship.

Although Chacel describes herself as a slow writer, her production is considerable: the four novels that followed *Leticia Valle;* a volume of 'unfinished' novels and several collections of poems, short stories, and essays; two major works of nonfiction, *La confesión* (Confession) and *Saturnal* (Saturnalia); a biography of her husband (who died in 1977); *Desde el amanecer* and two volumes of her diary; and numerous essays and translations from English, French, and Italian. For many years her work was virtually unknown in Spain, where the Generation of '27, to which she belongs by birth, became known as a generation of poets — and of men. Like that of María Zambrano, the philosopher (1904–91), and other women who have been accorded even less recognition, Chacel's work has only recently begun to receive the sustained critical attention it merits. Serious interest in her was first evidenced in Spain in the early 1960s: she returned for a brief visit in 1962; a new edition of *Teresa* was published there in 1963, and young writers in Barcelona who had begun to read her novels established contact with her. Since Chacel's return to Spain, she has become known as a major Spanish writer; her work has been the subject of numerous studies, and she appears frequently in national literary forums. In 1987 she was awarded the prestigious Premio Nacional de Letras Españolas, and her books have been translated into several languages.[2] Chacel continues to live in Madrid with her son and daughter-in-law and to write daily.

With respect to the 'events' of her life, Chacel has said she would place herself 'in the margin,' and she has insisted repeatedly that her memory for dates and facts is abysmal. Placing her as a writer, however, is neither a difficult task nor a marginal one, since what she refers to as her 'project' has been consistent since the 1920s and the writing of *Estación:* the renovation of Spanish prose, an undertaking begun in a spirit of collaboration with the ideas of Ortega and her colleagues from that period.

Despite personal differences with some of those colleagues, including Ortega himself, and despite what she terms the defection of others, Chacel has remained faithful to that project and to the goals set in the period of her earliest work — between the time she first left Madrid for Rome and her departure with her son Carlos during the Civil War in 1936. This is especially true concerning the years in Rome, when she was physically distant from Spain but thoroughly immersed in the artistic experimentation taking place there. Those years have remained a beginning for her, which she resolutely considers her present.

2. 'MEMORIAS DE LETICIA VALLE' was begun while Rosa Chacel was living in Paris but not completed until she was in South America. The first portion, however, crossed the Atlantic before she did, after the well-known Argentine essayist and 'woman of letters' Victoria Ocampo asked Chacel if she would like to contribute something to *Sur*, the literary journal Ocampo had founded in 1931. Since its publication, the novel has been one of Chacel's most widely read works. There have been several Spanish editions since it first appeared in Spain in 1971, and it has been translated into French, German, and Portuguese. In 1971 a film based on *Leticia Valle* was made by Spanish director Miguel Angel Rivas. Chacel collaborated on the script, but she was not pleased with the results, and the film was not a commercial success.

As Chacel has described it over the course of several interviews, the idea for *Leticia Valle* occurred to her long before she actually started to write the novel.[3] That 'idea' was both literary and factual in origin. While she was living in Rome, she learned in conversation about a young girl in one of Dostoevsky's novels who committed suicide after being seduced by a much older man, and that episode reminded her of a scandal that had exploded in a small Spanish town where the schoolteacher had seduced a little girl. Together, Chacel says, those two incidents prompted her to conceive of 'a novel in which a thirteen-year-old girl would seduce an older man and he would be the one who had to commit suicide.'[4]

The anecdote from Dostoevsky (which Ana Rodríguez has traced to Stavrogin's confession in *The Possessed*),[5] is not the only literary 'refraction' that contributed to *Leticia Valle*'s composition. More than traces can be found, for example, of the admiration Chacel has often mentioned for Dámaso Alonso's translation of James Joyce's *Portrait of the Artist as a Young Man* and the deep interest with which she read translations of Proust's fiction and Freud's early essays.[6] The presence of José Zorrilla is explicit in the quotations from 'La carrera' (The race). Through that poem another poet is present as well: Chacel claims that when she was a child, Zorrilla's poem about a Moorish king caused her to fall in love with Juan Ramón Jiménez, the Nobel Prize-winning poet born in 1881. What is more, Chacel has noted that *Leticia Valle*'s Daniel 'looked exactly like Juan Ramón,' and that Jiménez had once even fallen in love with a very young girl.[7]

Finally, although less explicitly and in spite of the independent direction Chacel has stressed for *Leticia Valle*, José Ortega y Gasset and his aesthetics were crucial in the formulation of Leticia's struggle to understand what has happened to her and the extent of her complicity in it. In the conceptualization of the novel, in the structure of its incidents, and in Leticia's own raw 'brute force' (*la fuerza bruta*), there are more than hints of both the energy Chacel admired in Ortega and the abrasion between them she has recalled in several of her essays. In this regard, I would mention Ortega's call, in *Meditaciones del Quijote* (Meditations on Don Quijote), for a novel in which description itself was predominant, rather than the thing or experience described. I would also mention Daniel's arrogance and the humiliation Leticia suffers as his pupil, noting a resemblance between some of their interchanges and Chacel's description of her meetings with Ortega.[8]

3. SIMANCAS was not present in Chacel's earliest plans for *Leticia Valle*, and its appearance when the novel was published marks one of the few changes between the book and the short piece published in *Sur*. This slight but significant alteration changed the context and the scope of Leticia's story dramatically.

In the original version, Leticia and her family leave Valladolid for Sardón de Duero; the intention was for Leticia to become involved with the schoolteacher there. Chacel had explained that in planning the novel she was thinking of Santibáñez de Valcova, the small town where the specific incident she remembered had taken place (García Valdés, 27). By the time *Leticia Valle* was completed, however, Sardón de Duero had become Simancas, and the schoolteacher was an archivist.

The importance of the change and the role of Simancas cannot be exaggerated, because of the role played by the village and its Archive in Spanish history and culture. Situated on a small hill that afforded valuable perspective and protection in an otherwise flat area, the fortress and surrounding village now known as Simancas date back to the fifth century B.C. An important site for both Romans and Goths, it was also pivotal during the Reconquest (722–1492), when the town became an outpost between the Christian north and the Islamic south. Subsequently, as a marker between the kingdoms of Leon and Castile and between lands held by the Castilian counts and those of their king, Simancas continued to be associated with a frontier until the end of the eleventh century. By that time the frontier of the Reconquest had moved, and Valladolid, a new town not far from Simancas, was growing in importance. Simancas was soon subsumed under its jurisdiction, although the village retained some of its privileges because of its loyalty to the Castilian king in his feuds with the local nobles.

In the late fifteenth century a castle was constructed from the ancient fortress by Admiral D. Alonso Enríquez, whose domains included the village. That castle soon passed into the hands of the Catholic Kings; it has belonged to the Spanish state ever since, and over the centuries Simancas has remained a small village. During the reign of Charles I (Charles V of the Holy Roman Empire), when Valladolid was the Spanish capital, the castle in Simancas seemed an ideal repository for official documents; it served as the state archives until 1859. At that time, the Archivo Nacional Histórico was created in Madrid to house current government papers. This meant that the Archivo General in Simancas became a 'closed' collection to which no further records would be added. The castle has continued to be an active 'Fortress of History,' however, and the wealth of its holdings — which include centuries' worth of documentation from Europe and the Americas — attracts scholars from all over the world.

In recent times, the fact that the Archive in Simancas was located in a small village, isolated from both Madrid and Valladolid, created a paradoxical situation of historical wealth and intellectual impoverishment. This was especially true for the late nineteenth- and early twentieth-century archivist whose fate it was to be stationed in such an out-of-the-way place, an educated practitioner of a newly created profession. In fact, in early twentieth-century Spain, at the time the story of *Leticia Valle* takes place, the archivist of Simancas was effectively cut off from the rich historical and cultural life symbolized by the castle. It was not until 1927 that daily automobile service between Valladolid and Simancas was established for researchers and not until 1930 that the archivist was permitted to reside in Valladolid rather than Simancas. For a couple like Daniel and Luisa, who found themselves in Simancas after having lived in Seville (and, implicitly, being associated with the Archivo General de Indias located there), the assignment would have been most difficult.[9]

4. JOSÉ ZORRILLA Y MORAL (1817–93) is not likely to be a name well known to readers in English, despite their familiarity with the protagonist of his famous play, *Don Juan Tenorio* (1844). That the case is quite different for Spanish readers is clear from the discussion in *Leticia Valle* between Luisa and the doctor about whether Leticia should recite one of Zorrilla's poems. And in fact, *Leticia Valle*'s English-language reader might not need to have any further information about this poet. Several things seem worth noting, however, because they are common knowledge to most Spanish readers and because, like Simancas, their contribution to the novel is inseparable from Leticia's circumstance.

In the first place, Zorrilla is not only an 'important' Spanish poet; he is one of the most famous of Spanish poets. Known throughout the Spanish-speaking world for *Don Juan Tenorio*, he was 'the national poet of the nineteenth century' and 'the last major poet of the Romantic period . . . [who] made the Romantic movement popular and respectable.'[10] Zorrilla was also known for his 'legends' (*leyendas*), 'legendary tales performed on a medieval scaffolding, at once Oriental, Moorish, and Christian.'[11] He was particularly interested in Spain's Moorish legacy, which he evoked vividly in poems such as 'La carrera' as noble and heroic.

The complex role of 'La carrera' in *Leticia Valle* and the related presence of the Moor(s) in the rest of the novel deserves a full-length study. There is of course the triumph of Leticia's recitation, and the power of the spoken word and the oral — as opposed to the written — tradition. But there is more. While the castle and Archive evoke the Reconquest and the preservation of Spanish (that is, Castilian, not Islamic) history and official heritage, the poem exonerates the Moor to the point of eulogy. Daniel, the custodian of the national past in his role as archivist, suggests to Leticia the Old Testament figure in the lions' den, but he resembles as well a Moorish king from the first time she sees him. And her father, implicitly a 'pure' Spaniard, has served in Africa (where he went to the Rif 'to get himself killed by the Moors').

Although no specific dates appear in *Leticia Valle*, the portrait of Alfonso XIII (ruled 1902–31) that Leticia sees at the celebration places the novel in the first decades of this century. Other references and remarks suggest that Colonel Valle fought during the Moroccan crisis of 1909. In that year, reservists were called up for a highly unpopular 'minor campaign . . . to defend Moroccan mining concessions.'[12] The campaign provoked a national strike and prefigured the humiliating defeat Spain's army would see in Morocco some years later. One can look forward and back with respect to *Leticia Valle* and Spanish history. Looking back, it is not difficult to discern a suggestion of the many *romances* (ballads) associated with the Moorish invasion of 711 and the legendary seduction that occasioned it. As those ballads tell it, King Roderick (el rey Rodrigo) of Toledo was overpowered by Moorish generals enlisted by Count Julián, the Visogothic governor of Ceuta, who called on them when he learned from his daughter—whom he had sent to be educated at Roderick's court—that she had been seduced by the king.[13] Looking forward a few years from 1909, it is not difficult to discern the presence of more troops from Africa and the outbreak of the Civil War.

Finally, to return to Zorrilla, like Leticia and like Chacel herself the poet was born in Valladolid. In fact, as Chacel explains in *Desde el amanecer*, Zorrilla's second wife was Chacel's great-aunt (27–28). Her maternal grandfather was a close friend of

Zorrilla, and the women the two men married were sisters. Zorrilla, according to Chacel, was a significant figure in her childhood. When the family lived in Valladolid, her parents staged plays for her in her room, and works by Zorrilla were her favorites. She also notes something even more important for her aesthetic education when she describes the disenchantment she experienced as she looked at a statue of Zorrilla in the park. Although she acknowledges that at the time she could not have put her feelings into words, she has precise memories of reflecting on that figure on a pedestal and comparing Zorrilla's prosaic pose, linked to her familiar, familial knowledge of him, with the ornate solemnity of a public statue. She likens her experience to the thoughts one has in front of a formal portrait of a person who looks less than imposing (26–27).

5. PORTRAITS and resemblance, or the lack of it, are crucial for a reading of *Leticia Valle*, in several ways. Most immediately, within the incidents of the novel and Leticia's narration, the portrait of Daniel in the lions' den that slips from the pages of Leticia's notebook prompts Daniel to admonish his pupil that the likeness she finds between the two figures is erroneous. Daniel will not defeat his lions, no matter what she thinks. Nor is this the only instance when Leticia's perception of how things 'are' proves to be skewed. On the contrary, she herself complains of how difficult it is to know exactly what people are talking about, exactly what is 'happening' around her. This mystery, in fact, is perhaps her principal complaint about childhood: instead of real guidance, she points out, one is given trivialized explanations in which truth is wrapped in misleading words. No wonder, then, she might say, that a person would be wrong about someone like Daniel, that I would know so little about my mother, that I would have to spy on my father to find out why his speech was consistently slurred while we were eating.

In a wider context, with respect to Chacel's writing of *Leticia Valle*, Joyce's *Portrait of the Artist* could be discussed at length.[14] It would also be worth pursuing the many associations between *Leticia Valle*, Chacel's comments about the novel's composition, and *Desde el amanecer.* Since such studies are not the purpose of these glosses, I will not speculate about the extent to which *Leticia Valle* is or is not autobiographical.[15] I do want, however, to note two instances in which Chacel addressed this issue, albeit indirectly. The first and less indirect allusion was in a conversation I had with her in the summer of 1991. She and I were discussing, with her son and daughter-in-law, whether a photograph of Chacel herself as a young girl would be an appropriate cover for *Leticia Valle*, or whether it would suggest that the novel was not fiction but autobiography. Our consensus went against using the photograph; the novel is not autobiographical, Chacel stressed, 'although it is a portrait of me.'[16] (I should add that this was not the first time Chacel had made a similar statement. In her conversation with García Valdés [26], for example, she told the interviewer that she was Leticia, although Leticia's story never happened to her.) The second reference occurred in another conversation in which Chacel was discussing *Leticia Valle* as the first novel on which she truly worked independently (that is, without responding directly to Ortega y Gasset). *Leticia Valle*, she explained, 'is my own, it is memories.'[17]

How those memories might be linked to the events recorded in *Desde el amanecer* is suggested by Chacel's recollection there of a little girl with whom she went to school in Valladolid. Chacel explains that she made no friends at the school and that she never spoke to the little girl. She remembers, though, that the child was beautiful and that she had the wonderful name of Leticia. The name, which does in fact derive from the Latin *laetitia* (joy), must have some sublime meaning, she thought, because it appeared in the litany. Chacel also liked the name because its color made her think of Snow White. She remembers that she had assigned a different color to each vowel, 'with as much conviction as Rimbaud.' 'Leticia' had two *i*'s (red) and an *a* (white), which led her to imagine two drops of blood on the snow, spilt by a queen (80).

'Valle,' that I know of, has never been explained. Perhaps it refers to Valladolid. Or perhaps it was meant to suggest—as it does to me—Ramón del Valle-Inclán (1866–1936), another Spanish writer, whom Chacel admired and knew personally. Valle-Inclán was also the author of some apocryphal memoirs, whose narrator, the Marqués de Bradomín, Leticia resembles rather remarkably in several ways. Bradomín, too, had an incestuous 'father-daughter' relationship (with his own daughter in *Sonata de invierno* [*Sonata of Winter*]), and like Leticia he withheld many of the most unpleasant things he had done.[18] Chacel, I might add, also omits from *Leticia Valle* at least one detail from her own 'true' story that she could have used—an incident (related to the name Leticia) about 'the worm of conscience' (*el gusanillo de la conciencia*), which she does include in *Desde el amanecer*. And it was omitted even though she thought of that phrase until she was thirty or forty years old, every time she experienced a 'convulsion' of conscience.

6. CONVULSION is my literal translation of *convulsión*. I have used it deliberately because the word leads directly to the portrait of Chacel I find in the novel (as well as in the associations with respect to 'Leticia' and 'Valle'). That portrait, or perhaps I should say the resemblance I find in it, would best be described as one of convulsion. In using the term, I am thinking of its usual connotations (contraction, upheaval, paroxysm; an emotion or experience that wrenches; a person contorted, struggling, writhing). I am also thinking of Chacel's use of 'convulsion' in one of her essays, where she employs it to describe

the phenomena of 'communication,' 'community,' and 'communion.' All those phenomena, she says, are merely 'convulsions of human unity . . . struggling for self-knowledge through a dialogue with the self.'[19] A thorough discussion of Chacel's dialogue — and of the way her unity is composed of a duality, of two that can give rise to three — would of course require more than a gloss. I introduce it nevertheless because of its association, for Chacel, with confession as opposed to memoirs. Memoirs, as she explains them in *La confesión*, are occasioned by an urge to remember and to tell or narrate; they involve reliving or redoing.[20] Confession, on the other hand, is linked not so much to remembering as to showing, to making manifest. In this way, according to Chacel, it is similar to a conclusion about human life that has arisen from what one has learned or seen. At the same time, however, because that conclusion involves bringing to light something new or previously unheard of, it is confessed as dialogue, upheaval, convulsion. It is also confessed with difficulty, since a new way of defending or presenting human life will by necessity break new ground.[21]

Where Chacel's portrait is most discernible in *Leticia Valle*, as I have come to recognize her through translating the novel and reading her other novels and essays, is in her confession of the 'conclusion' I find presented through Leticia's story. Put simply — and I do this at the risk of reduction but in an effort to understand Chacel in the same terms that she has used to understand the confession of others[22] — it is that Eros, or what she terms the erotic motion, is present in young children, both female and male, from the instant they are born. What is more, it is present with respect to no fixed object, and it is not synonymous with sexual desire or sexuality. Finally, as a force, it becomes crippled significantly when it is directed toward a specific end or confined to a fixed path.

Chacel's readings of Freud are more than evident in that

conclusion, and she invariably mentions them, both in discussing her early work and in her essays. In fact, she even argues strongly on Freud's behalf when she points out that perhaps only Saint Augustine could have understood Freud. Freud's 'purest, loftiest' discovery, she says — and one that she believes no one wants to grant him — is that 'the erotic motion . . . is undifferentiated toward everything and every beloved person.'[23] Her own interest in and application of Freud's discovery, however, veers from his as she explores it in her own context. That context, at least in *Leticia Valle*, is one of an exceptionally intelligent female child whose intense, undirected Eros or 'brute force' both propels her indiscriminately toward interesting, talented adults of both sexes and draws them to her.[24] At the same time, it also threatens those people. Leticia is not fully aware of the implications of her 'powers'; she inhabits a threshold where she hovers between innocence and awareness and between control and victimization.

By placing Leticia at a point of such ambivalence, it seems to me, Chacel is presenting or confessing her 'conclusion' about Eros according to Freud, but with her own very individual observations about the socialization of female children and in the probing, even interrogative way that is characteristic of all her writing. In that socialization, both men and women are shown to be complicit in the corralling and taming of Leticia's 'erotic motion' and her extraordinary abilities. At the same time, Leticia is shown to be not only affectionate and intelligent but headstrong and manipulative, as well as resilient to an extent that makes it difficult to ascribe blame to the adults around her without qualification. As she writes her final paragraphs, she is devastated, alone, and in tears. Yet she continues to eat, she knows she will sleep well, and the last word in her narrative harks back to her 'calculation.' There is, as Chacel has acknowledged (García Valdés, 28), something 'monstrous' about her, which Chacel likens to something in herself.[25] It is also something Chacel questions in *Leticia Valle*, confessing and defending it in a new way through Leticia, the 'brutishness' she is admonished to avoid, and the 'brute force' responsible for her survival.

7. BRUTISHNESS, its association with the trivialities of the 'world of women' (as opposed to the erudition of the 'world of men'), and its relation to the 'brute force' that sustains Leticia are aspects of her 'memoirs' that Leticia registers without understanding them fully. She resembles Chacel in that she too struggles with Eros, but she writes without comprehending that struggle, surprised at the tenacity of her own desire and its continuance after all that has happened to her. Although, to some extent, she controls her story, that control is limited to decisions about what she will withhold and what she will tell. She could not, for example, speculate about the 'brute force' of Eros and the siege to which that brute force is constantly subjected, as Chacel does in 'Esquema de los problemas prácticos y actuales del amor' (An outline of the practical and current problems concerning love), a long article published a few years before *Leticia Valle*.[26]

In 'Esquema,' Chacel writes not of love's metaphysics but of its 'historical fortune' (*ventura histórica*, 130). The task she identifies for herself (and her time) is one of 'establishing a perfect correlation between the essential notions we hold about love and our erotic procedures and reactions.'[27] Such a task, Chacel indicates, calls for a long hard look at behaviors that have more recently begun to be discussed in terms of gender, and at the work of leading (male) theorists who were her contemporaries. As Teresa Bordons and Susan Kirkpatrick have explained in their discussion of Chacel's novel *Teresa*, those theorists included Georg Simmel and C. G. Jung, both of whom argued for and enumerated qualitative differences between male and female psyches.[28] Chacel opposed that position, insisting that even when such definitions apparently prompt good will (in their praise of feminine spirituality, for example), in effect they condemn women to isolation, barring them from the realm of thought, erudition, and action (Simmel) or of the Logos (Jung). According to Chacel, the bifurcation of 'man' (*hombre*) as 'humanity' into 'men' and 'women' diminishes all human beings. Its effect on women is particularly adverse, however, since it ensures that their work will invariably be associated with the clever forms but impoverished interiors that are implicitly less 'human' than the achievements of men.

Chacel's concerns in 'Esquema' reappear in *Leticia Valle* in several ways. One of them, quite clearly, involves Leticia's recognition, when she becomes Daniel's pupil, that her lack of interest in studying and her fascination with the 'silliness' and 'petty vices' of women have resulted in an undeniable 'brutishness' on her part. The implications of that recognition, however, are even more far-reaching than Leticia indicates directly. Not only is an unmediated 'brute force' responsible for her survival at the end of the novel, but that force bears close resemblance to the erotic force or motion I have discussed with respect to Chacel's 'confession.' What Chacel 'confesses' as her 'conclusion' in *Leticia Valle* is the force of life, of Eros, in a young girl and the extent to which it both attracts (even magnetizes) those around her and is misunderstood, misdirected, and threatened by virtually every adult with whom she comes in contact.[29]

The nature of such a force, Chacel writes in 'Esquema,' is perceived as essentially criminal. Thoroughly promiscuous, it attaches itself without regard to prescribed norms but with unfailing enthusiasm and consistent 'infidelity.'[30] To harness it, she suggests, is to 'kill' it by bringing its 'transcendent responsibility' within lawful bounds' (174). This is a labor that actively, albeit often unwittingly, involves a concerted effort on the part of both men and women (177),[31] who must begin to restrain a child from the day he or she is born (170–80). At the same time, however, it is a labor that must operate in a doubly intense way in the case of women so as to ensure their continual subordination, the association of their 'brute force' with activities that seem insignificant, trivial, and 'brutish' when measured against the more 'vigorous' (that is, more intellectually and spiritually 'robust,' 178) activities of men. It hardly seems a coincidence that in 'Esquema' (140) Chacel discusses as implicitly synonymous Max Scheler's 'animality' and Simmel's 'femininity' with respect to the 'ecstatic state' that precedes consciousness.

Although there are individual passages in *Leticia Valle* in which the directness and clarity Chacel associates with memoirs tends to become blurred as a result of the tension and strain she identifies in confession (*La confesión*, 37–38), Leticia acknowledges her 'brute force' without truly questioning it. (In fact, the two genres are not, Chacel advises, always distinct [*La confesión*, 20]). Leticia's failure to do that, however, as well as her inability to relate it to the 'brutishness' she seeks to escape, her almost uncanny capacity for intense experience, and her ability to survive only strengthen the associations *Leticia Valle* suggests between (female) children, Eros, and the effects of the 'essential notions' about 'love and our erotic procedures and reactions' discussed in 'Esquema.' Leticia may be an unparalleled young woman, Chacel seems to imply, but look at what happens to her 'tremendous, ineffable force' as she is educated in her own home, in school, and in the home of Daniel and Luisa. Watch the destruction of the 'transcendent responsibility' in that force as Leticia learns to sew, as she tries to find out about her mother, as she observes her father's eccentric, bitter behavior, or as Luisa and Daniel vie for her allegiance.

181

8. IMPLICATION, so essential for both Chacel's novel and Leticia's narrative, could also be considered the key factor in the translation of *Leticia Valle*, and I want to discuss it here in three contexts.

The first has to do with difficulty. Because Leticia's narrative is highly allusive and because the many passages in which she recalls her thoughts are dense and convoluted, the novel is not an easy one to read. This is especially true at the beginning; Chacel has Leticia start to write with great effort, and for most readers the first few pages will only become clear, and perhaps only become interesting, after they have read the entire book. This is also true in sections where Leticia's use of language is allusive and her allusions to 'what happened' are so vague that one cannot be certain just what it is she might be trying to say. In such instances, a translator can choose to have Leticia speak (somewhat more) articulately and thus translate, as it were, the incidents of her story; or a translator can choose to have her speak (somewhat more) haltingly in order to translate Chacel's exploration of language through her protagonist. (The word 'choose' is important here, because the nature of translation is such that a translator *will* have to choose, or at least interpret and proceed accordingly; ideally, the choice is conscious and deliberate.) The former choice will give rise to a better 'read,' but I believe that the latter will ultimately convey Leticia's story more fully, because it will allow the reader to recognize the extent to which Chacel has linked Eros to her use of language, both spoken and written — a distinction that must be evident in the actual text — that is, the words — of her novel.

Those words are the second context of 'implication,' for even the unspoken aspects of Leticia's narrative imply her circumstance. Thus an urge to narrate is countered continually by a determination not to tell, just as Leticia's purpose of showing exactly what came of her 'lofty sentiments' is countered by a refusal to ask for sympathy or pity, and just as her continued life is countered by efforts to stand still. This countering, which could also be termed ambivalence, is evident not only in Leticia's withholding of information but also in the holding back evident in her words themselves. Although there are many sections of the novel where the narration flows easily, there are also passages in which Leticia's sentences are long and complex. They can always be deciphered, but on occasion the deciphering is slow and laborious, and even when deciphered, they clearly prove to be ambiguous. Once again, a translator's interpretation or reading involves a decision about Chacel's play with language. This means interpreting Leticia's unusually long sentences, her liberal use of colons and semicolons, and the way in which she repeats herself in her explanations, although always in different words. Chacel's critics have yet to study her use of language in *Leticia Valle*, but when they do, I suspect they will find their work well rewarded, and I believe they will document what I have sensed as a translator: that the convulsion registered in the incidents of Leticia's story is registered with equal intensity in her use of words themselves.

My third comment about implication concerns the unwritten elements of Leticia's story that are present continually in her narrative but never told in their entirety. Those elements include the events from her relationship with Daniel that she refuses to narrate and the details of her childish flirtation with the pharmacist's son who sang her the habanera (details she could not quite tell to Daniel). They also include both the numerous mysteries about Leticia's parents, which are never quite explained (and whose explanations Leticia does not possess), and incidents like the one with her mother in which Leticia is involved but without being able to evaluate them fully. This last example is particularly interesting because it suggests a complex, ambiguous relationship between Leticia and the one real love she has known. A curious shift of position in the incident with her mother suggests that Leticia voluntarily separated herself from her mother in order to enjoy more thoroughly (at a distance, through memory and its re-presentation) the pleasure of experiencing their bodies fused as one. On the one hand that shift points to the absolute 'infidelity' of the erotic motion and an individual's 'brute force' as Chacel portrays them through Leticia. On the other, like the many silences in the novel, it serves to draw the reader into Leticia's narrative, through struggle or difficulty rather than accessibility. 'I try for the impossible,' Chacel has explained in referring to her first novel, 'to make the reader understand what I do not even mention.'[32]

9. THE IMPOSSIBLE for Chacel, then, coincides with Leticia's inability (whether from unwillingness or sheer incapacity) to describe certain incidents. At the same time, however, it is distinct from that inability. In fact, Chacel's 'try for the impossible' is successful only to the extent that Leticia makes *her* limits as a narrator explicit and convincing.

I have discussed that paradox in the preceding gloss, but I want to return to it briefly because Chacel's use of language in Leticia's narrative has proved to be one of the most challenging and absorbing aspects of translating *Leticia Valle*. To discuss it, one must work with the smallest units of translation and scrutinize Leticia's sentences and her words. As that scrutiny occurs (and it must occur in translation, even though words and sentences are neither the only nor the ultimate units of translation), what becomes evident is not only the continued tension between the different implications of Leticia's 'I cannot' (I refuse? I do not have the skill? I am not permitted?) but also the imprecision of her words themselves.

Leticia has a large vocabulary for a twelve-year-old, and her ability to navigate her way through syntactical structures is impressive. Her confusion about the events in which she has participated, however, is demonstrated repeatedly by her lack of precision when it comes to the most disturbing of her experiences, in particular by the limited number of words she has for referring to them. One example is the consistently imprecise way in which she speaks of 'what happened' without ever specifying the 'what.' The same could be said about her other fantasies and 'diversions.' What exactly went through her head at those times, which she describes more in terms of the torment they cause her as she remembers them than of their incidents? What might link her daydreams about the Beer King, her fantasies as she looks at the sun shining through the fabric of Daniel's shirt on the skin of his chest, her wish to see a sword in Luisa's hand? What exactly does she remember when she says that she should have told Daniel about her 'past' so that he could have been on his guard about her?

As a translator, my response to those questions would be not to answer them but to draw attention to Leticia's singular use of language. At once imprecise and highly allusive, her frequently unexplained 'erotic' experiences not only situate her on the threshold of adolescence but make the reader experience her confusion and her limited ability either to define those experiences or account for them satisfactorily. In this way, Leticia's inadequate vocabulary forces the reader to imagine, to fill in the details by putting words in her mouth or on her page, just as some of her lengthy sentences force the reader to decide exactly what Leticia 'means' to say. Such decisions, I might add, also force a reader to participate in the previously 'inconceivable' nature of Leticia's fantasies themselves and in a series of events recounted with the hesitancy one might expect from an inexperienced narrator with such an unconventional perspective.

10. CHIAROSCURO was at first titled 'feminism,' but the more I thought about it, the more I decided that what I wanted to note

about women and *Leticia Valle* would follow better from a different point of departure.

Toward the end of the novel, Leticia studies Luisa as Luisa talks with two women from Simancas who have come to visit her. As she notes that one of the women has totally misunderstood a remark made by Luisa, Leticia observes a succession of small grimaces appearing on Luisa's face, which has always seemed completely serene to her. At that moment she realizes that what she perceived as Luisa's impassivity was invariable only because the changes registered in Luisa's expression had been too subtle for her to recognize. She likens this experience to her searches for pine cones, which were invisible in the grass until she learned to spot 'the chiaroscuro that gave them away.'

It seems to me that 'chiaroscuro' is a particularly apt word for referring to the portraits of women Chacel draws in *Leticia Valle*. In fact, the only equally appropriate one that comes to mind is 'meditation,' especially if one uses it with a thought to the refractions and multiple perspectives in Ortega's *Meditaciones del Quijote*. For what Chacel offers in her novel could be described as a meditation in chiaroscuro on the coming of age of a young child. Although that young child is biologically female, at first 'she' is no more she than he: Leticia is drawn to adults who attract her because of their skill and intelligence, and if she disdains women and little girls, it is because they are engaged in gossip, and whatever they do seems trivial. At the same time, however, women are not shown to be simply victims any more than they are shown to be marginal. Quite the contrary, as Chacel has explained in her essays, women have been enslaved repeatedly, but they have also been complicit in that enslavement (I am thinking here particularly of 'La mujer en galeras' [Women as galley slaves], although, as I have indicated with respect to 'convulsion,' these ideas were at work in Chacel's thinking as early as 'Esquema.' This means, as Chacel has indicated frequently, that they have been very much at the center of things.

Since Chacel's examination of those 'things' frequently occurs from a woman's point of view, it is not surprising that her critics have wanted to discuss her work in terms of feminism. This is particularly true in interview situations, where time after time Chacel has refused emphatically to define herself as a feminist, stressing a definition of 'man' that includes men and women and the need for women to claim a culture to which they have traditionally been given only restricted access but in which they have participated fully, not only as 'slaves' but as perpetuators. No doubt her suggestion to women would be — and this can be glimpsed in *Leticia Valle* — not to deny 'masculine' achievements but to incorporate them and master them in such a way that they also embody 'feminine' strengths. Thus, despite Chacel's scrutiny of women's subordination and her determination to prompt an understanding of events that exceeds and at times even mocks the limits of written language, it would be inappropriate to focus a discussion of her work solely on 'women's issues.' In his remarks on *Leticia Valle*, Luis Antonio de Villena refers to Chacel's desire to 'find the best kind of femininity in intelligent manliness' and to Leticia's intuition that 'the perfect woman would have to be a man.'[33] Villena may be overstating his case by overlooking the extent to which *Leticia Valle* invites a revaluation of the education and socialization of a young woman. At the same time, however, he does point to Chacel's continued refusal of any efforts to define or create a separate 'feminine' identity. This suggests, for example, as Reyes Lázaro has indicated, that even certain coincidences between Chacel's use of language and the work of such feminist theorists, writers, and thinkers as Luce Irigaray and Julia Kristeva might best be seen as simply that: instances of coincidence rather than true convergence.[34]

'If I seem "machista" to you, you might be right,' Chacel told one North American interviewer,[35] and I can imagine that there will be readers of *Leticia Valle* in English who will be inclined to criticize her as such. For my part, I would be inclined to leave open for further study the possibility that Chacel's use of language and her strategies vis-à-vis canonical (male) writers may prove to be more harmonious with 'feminist' thinking than critics have heretofore recognized. Thus I would agree with Abigail Six, who has written a very thoughtful article on *Desde el amanecer.* 'Her comments,' Six has observed about Chacel's discussion of the creation of a work of art, 'are only superficially masculine in approach.' This observation leads Six to discuss ways in which Chacel's work 'intersects with feminist theory' and to indicate points of agreement and separation' (86–87). Six too uses the word 'chiaroscuro' in her comments about Chacel's 'refusal to align these [feminine] categories with positive and negative, with soft and hard, with warm and cold' (87). By praising what she terms the 'chiaroscuro effect,' Six emphasizes the subtlety of Chacel's work and its complexity.[36] With respect to *Leticia Valle*, I would add that the 'chiaroscuro effect' should be extended to include not only the 'effect' 'facing' the reader but the activity into which that reader is drawn. By presenting Leticia's narrative as a monologue-dialogue that Leticia sustains with herself and by pacing that monologue-dialogue slowly and deliberately, Chacel requires the reader, who inevitably becomes Leticia's interlocutor, to participate actively in a situation of intense ambivalence, to look closely at the pine cones hidden in the grass.

'Feminism' or 'feminist,' then, with respect to *Leticia Valle*, can be used only with considerable qualification, and they are perhaps best not used at all. On the other hand, to consider the questions Chacel's work raises about masculinity and femininity is to question and problematize those terms. It is also, perhaps, to reflect on 'feminism' and 'feminist' as words that may be less international than some critics and translators acknowledge. 'If I seem 'machista' to you,' Chacel could have said, 'it may be that we're using the same word but speaking different languages.' Rather than a dictionary equivalent, the translation of those languages often requires an explanation or a parallel term.

11. PARALLELS are crucial for translators, who look for similar texts that 'have been produced in more or less identical situations.'[37] As originally written by Albrecht Neubert, that statement refers to the translation of nonliterary texts, but I have found it helpful in working with literary texts as well, because it allows me to visualize translation as an activity of contiguity rather than substitution. Richard Sieburth has written of 'the communion of simple adjacency' that he has experienced between a text and its translation,[38] and his description also strikes me as instructive. It differs from my definition of parallel texts insofar as the importance translators should accord to likeness is concerned, but both sentences suggest that not only resemblance but its lack (and perhaps even its opposite) are at play in a successful translation. Sieburth also writes of 'one language sharing a moment of silence with another,'[39] which seems a particularly apt description for *Leticia Valle*, where what a translator would most want to convey is the highly verbal silence engulfing the incidents that occasioned Leticia's narration.

What texts might be parallel to *Leticia Valle?* Certainly the texts either written in Spanish or translated into Spanish that Chacel has mentioned as ones she read with interest before or during the composition of her third novel. Further suggestions would be novels written in Spanish at about the same time, such as Carmen Laforet's *Nada* (*Andrea*), which is also narrated by a young woman and was published in the same year as *Leticia Valle*. Mario Parajón, for example, has placed *Leticia Valle* by discussing it in relation not only to Sartre's *La nausée* but also to

Nada and novels by Spaniard Pío Baroja, Cuban Lino Novás Calvo, and Argentine Adolfo Bioy Casares — all published in 1945.[40] *La familia de Pascual Duarte* (*The family of Pasqual Duarte*), published in 1942 by the Nobel Prize-winning writer Camilo José Cela (b. 1916), would be another parallel text written in Spain and another text marked by the Civil War, although, like *Leticia Valle*, it takes place earlier. Yet another, and one quite close to *Leticia Valle* in many ways, is *Delirio y destino* (Delirium and destiny), a novel published in 1989 by Spanish philosopher María Zambrano (1904–91) shortly before her death. Written in Cuba in the early 1950s, Zambrano's novel is a highly autobiographical *Bildungsroman* in which a young woman relates her coming to awareness under Ortega's tutelage during the decade of the 1920s.

Although Chacel has yet to be studied in an international context, numerous parallels come to mind in addition to those of Dostoevsky, Joyce, and Proust, which Chacel has indicated herself; I would mention Virginia Woolf and Simone de Beauvoir, both of whom Chacel has discussed in her essays, as well as Gertrude Stein and Marguerite Duras. Vladimir Nabokov's *Lolita* will also come to mind because of its date as well as the age of its protagonist.[41] I would place *Lolita* in a list of texts *Leticia Valle* might be said to subvert, however, recalling Chacel's observation that a new conclusion about human life will inevitably present that life in a new way. In a full study of *Leticia Valle*, the novel would have to be considered in company with other tales of sexually precocious young girls adored and described by older men. It would also have to be discussed in relation to other volumes of memoirs, most of which would also be written by men, although I suspect that such a study would ultimately uncover more parody than parallels. One of the things unparalleled about *Leticia Valle* is that Leticia speaks rather than Daniel, even though her speech is often halting.

Two other sorts of parallel texts must be mentioned here, both of which I would consider close to *Leticia Valle*—despite differences in incident or date of composition—because each of them involves narratives by young women about the age of Leticia. The first such narratives are diaries written by twelve-year-old girls: Anaïs Nin's first diary, written in French and begun in 1914 when Nin was eleven; and the diary of Anne Frank, written in German and begun in 1942 when Frank had just turned thirteen. The fact that neither of those diaries was originally written in English limits their usefulness with respect to a translator's choice of specific words (at least with respect to the translator's need to imagine how a twelve-year-old girl might write, or how a writer creating a twelve-year-old narrator would have her write). The manner of thinking of those young girls is helpful, however, especially in regard to its intensity and the topics the girls think about; also helpful is the way reflections of great seriousness alternate in their diaries with almost childlike passages. Leticia's narrative, too, is uneven, and I believe a translation should respect that unevenness, even if its inconsistency occurs in a different way, or in different passages.

The second type of such narratives are, like *Leticia Valle*, apocryphal first-person accounts: Georgia Savage's *The House Tibet* (1989) and Dorothy Allison's *Bastard out of Carolina* (1992). The explicitness of those narratives by young girls who have been raped by older men (a father in one case and a stepfather in another) sets them apart from *Leticia Valle*, however. It also prompts a certain historical consideration on the part of the translator: published in English in 1993, *Leticia Valle* will inevitably bear the mark of that date, yet it also bears the mark of the years in which it was written and those in which it takes place. When one thinks of parallels, then, one must think simultaneously: turn-of-the-century Spain as recalled by a young girl banished to Switzerland; Madrid, Paris, and Rio de Janeiro in the late 1930s and early 1940s; and Kent, Ohio, 1991 to 1993. In each retelling, Leticia's story will of necessity be told differently even as it remains consistent; in each retelling, Leticia must struggle with her own lack of understanding in such a way that she conveys her circumstance, a circumstance that includes by definition, no matter when it recurs, the impossibility of describing what happened.

12. 'DON' AND 'DOÑA' are Spanish terms of respect and formality used with an individual's given name. Strictly speaking, they cannot be translated into a language that lacks similar forms of address. This explains why they are often omitted in translation, even though they are an integral part of the relationships that exist between speakers of Spanish. I have retained them because I consider them an important aspect of Leticia's impossibility. When Leticia first meets the archivist and his wife, they are don Daniel and doña Luisa to her. This is as one would expect. Her relationship with the couple is immediately intimate enough that she would not refer to them as *señor* and *señora* (Mr. and Mrs.); indeed, their surnames are never used in the novel. On the other hand, it would be inappropriate for her to address them directly by their given names, any more than she would speak to them in the second-person familiar, the intimate form of 'you' (*tú*). There is no indication that this ever changes: following convention, Daniel and Luisa address Leticia in the familiar, and she responds in the formal. Leticia's practice does undergo a change, however, when Luisa asks her not to call her 'doña Luisa' any longer. As she has previously told Leticia's aunt, she considers Leticia her best friend, and she wants that friendship to be reflected in their conversation. Leticia complies, with some effort, and during the second half of the novel she speaks of Luisa and don Daniel—Daniel's title is never dropped, even in her thoughts about him, despite the increasing intimacy of their relationship.

The decision to retain *don* and *doña* is also related to other elements of my translation and to my general preference for a translation that is not 'transparent.' Although I believe that Leticia's story can be retold at any time and in any language, I also believe that every telling of it, whether in Bern or Paris or Rio de Janeiro or Kent, will, to a greater or lesser degree, take place in Simancas around 1910, where Leticia's day follows the traditional Spanish pattern in which 'dinner' is the midday meal (served between 2:00 and 3:00), children return to school in the late afternoon, and the evening ends with 'supper' before one goes to bed. This means that those retelling will invariably be 'hybrids,' as necessary elements of Leticia's narrative find their way relatively unaltered into a new context. To pretend otherwise is to compromise a story by limiting it to its incidents and stressing those incidents unduly. In Leticia's case that would be particularly risky, since so many of the incidents are present only by implication.

13. GLOSS is the word I have chosen to name my comments because it seemed appropriate for describing remarks I hoped would serve as both a finish for my work and a point of departure for further translation as *Leticia Valle* is read and interpreted in English. Although they are not as numerous as the glosses that complement M. F. K. Fisher's translation of Brillat-Savarin's *Physiology of Taste*, Fisher's engaging annotations were very much in my mind as I planned this afterword. Those annotations are both sequential and keyed to particular words or passages. My comments have also followed a sequence, but their references have not been to specific places in the novel; rather, the numbering corresponds loosely to a progression from the strictly informative to the more speculative. My interest, however, is consistently that of practice, and a definition of 'translation' as an activity of multiple mediations or 'refractions' that includes both 'translator' and 'reader.' Ultimately, I do not

believe there is any such 'thing' as a translation, any more than ultimately, there are texts or authors. Rather, one translates, reads, writes.

Finally, it seems fitting that these last words of 'finishing' be an expression of thanks to those friends and colleagues who have helped in various ways as I worked on this translation of *Leticia Valle:* Maryanne Bertram and Fred Maier, who read and commented on the manuscript in its entirety; Noël Valis and Roberta Salper, who read and commented on individual sections; Ana Fuentes and Amalia Magán, who answered questions about Spanish usage and expressions; Susan Kirkpatrick, who encouraged me to propose the project to the University of Nebraska Press; Antonio Piedra, who provided valuable orientation during my visit to Valladolid; and Ana Rodríguez-Fischer, who graciously spoke with me about Rosa Chacel and made available to me several as yet unpublished essays. I have learned from all of these people and incorporated their suggestions to the best of my ability. My gratitude goes as well to Research and Sponsored Programs at Kent State University for support that enabled me to meet Rosa Chacel in the summer of 1991 and to get to know Valladolid and Simancas firsthand.

I also want to thank Rosa Chacel for her willingness to speak with me and answer my questions about *Leticia Valle.* To her, I would say about translating *Leticia Valle* into English what she once wrote about translating Racine's *Phèdre* into Spanish: 'The undertaking is undeniably difficult, but once you get started, the work provides so much pleasure that all thoughts of difficulty disappear.'[42]

Notes

1. Very little biographical information about Chacel is available in English. The most extensive summary of her life and work is in Janet Pérez's *Contemporary Women Writers of Spain* (Boston: Twayne, 1988), 61–68. In Spanish, the best sources, in addition to numerous interviews and *Desde el amanecer* (Madrid: Revista de Occidente, 1972), are the following: *Timoteo Pérez Rubio y sus retratos en el jardín*, Chacel's biography of her husband (Madrid: Cátedra, 1980); the two volumes of her diary, *Alcancía. Ida* and *Alcancía. Vuelta* (Barcelona: Seix Barral, 1982); and her essays, especially 'Sendas perdidas de la Generación del 27,' *Cuadernos Hispanoamericanos* 322–23 (1977): 5–34 (rpt. in *Rebañaduras*, ed. Moisés Mori [Valladolid: Junta de Castilla y León, 1986], 91–128). In addition, a collection of letters to Chacel, edited by Ana Rodríguez-Fischer, has been published recently (*Cartas a Rosa Chacel* [Madrid: Cátedra/Versal, 1992]).

2. *Memoirs of Leticia Valle* is the second of Chacel's novels to appear in English. *The Maravillas District* (*Barrio de maravillas*), translated by d.a. démers, was published by the University of Nebraska Press in 1992.

3. My sources for these comments about *Leticia Valle* are primarily the remarks Chacel made in two interviews: Gema Vidal and Ruth Zauner, 'Rosa Chacel: La pasión de la perfección,' *Camp de l'Arpa* (Barcelona) 74 (April 1980): 69–73; and Olvido García Valdés, 'Conversación con Rosa Chacel,' *Un Angel Más* (Valladolid) 3–4 (1988): 15–43. Further references to García Valdés are given in parentheses in the text.

4. 'Una novela en que sea una niña de trece años la que seduzca a un señor y sea éste quien se tenga que colgar' (Vidal and Zauner, 'Rosa Chacel,' 72). I am responsible for this and all other translations in the 'Glosses.'

5. Cited by Shirley Mangini in her edition of Chacel's *Estación. Ida y vuelta* (Madrid: Cátedra, 1989), 81.

6. Chacel has described her reading of these writers on several occasions. The

fullest commentary is perhaps that in 'Sendas perdidas' (Mori, *Rebañaduras*, esp. 102).

7. 'Era Juan Ramón exactamente' (García Valdés, 'Conversación,' 27).

8. For Chacel's comments on those meetings, see her essay 'Ortega,' *Revista de Occidente* 24–25 (May 1983): 77–94. For a discussion in English of Chacel's relationship with Ortega, see Teresa Bordons and Susan Kirkpatrick, 'Chacel's *Teresa* and Ortega's Canon,' ALEC 19 (1992): 283–99; and Elizabeth Scarlett, 'Rosa Chacel, Ortega y Gasset, and Bodily Discourse,' *España Contemporánea* 5.1 (1992): 21–39.

9. For my information about Simancas I am indebted to Amando Represa's booklet *Simancas: Fortaleza de la historia* (Valladolid: Caja de Ahorros Popular de Valladolid, 1988). I am also grateful to María-Teresa Triguero Rodríguez and María Gloria Tejada from the Archivo General de Simancas for their help and conversation.

10. Willis Barnstone, ed. *Spanish Poetry: From Its Beginnings through the Nineteenth Century* (New York: Oxford University Press, 1970), 459. Barnestone's short discussion provides a good introduction in English to Zorrilla's work. To the best of my knowledge, 'La carrera' has never been translated into English. There are translations of several other poems, however, in James Kennedy's *Modern Poets and Poetry of Spain* (London: Longman, Brown, Green, & Longmans, 1852), and they were helpful to me as I prepared my translation.

11. Barnstone, *Spanish Poetry*, 459.

12. Raymond Carr, *Spain 1808–1975*, 2d ed. (New York: Oxford University Press, Clarendon Press, 1982), 483.

13. *Spanish Ballads*, ed. C. Colin Smith (Oxford: Pergamon Press, 1964), 51–59, provides a good discussion in English of these *romances*.

14. Two articles in Spanish that address the relationship between Chacel and Joyce are María J. Crespo Allúe and Luisa F. Rodríguez Palomero, '*A Portrait of the Artist as Young Man*, su traducción y Rosa Chacel,' *James Joyce Actas/Proceedings: Symposio Internacional en el Centenario de James Joyce* (Seville: Universidad de Sevilla, 1982), 67–85; and Aurora Egido, 'Los espacios del tiempo en *Memorias de Leticia Valle* de Rosa Chacel,' *Revista de Literatura* 43 (1981): 107–31.

15. Two critical discussions of this question are Kathleen M. Glenn, 'Fiction and Autobiography in Rosa Chacel's *Memorias de Leticia Valle*,' *Letras Peninsulares* 4.2–3 (1991): 285–94; and Luis Antonio de Villena, '*Memorias de Leticia Valle*: La seducción inversa,' in *Rosa Chacel: Premio Nacional de las Letras Españolas* (Madrid: Biblioteca Nacional, 1989), 41–44. Villena's essay appeared originally as the introduction to an edition of *Leticia Valle* published in 1987 (Barcelona: Círculo de Lectores).

16. 'Es un retrato de mí' (Rosa Chacel, personal conversation, 21 June 1991).

17. 'Es una cosa mía, son recuerdos' (Kathleen Glenn, 'Conversación con Rosa Chacel,' *Letras Peninsulares* 3.1 [1990]: 20).

18. I have discussed at length the relationship between *Leticia Valle* and *Sonata de invierno* in 'Siting *Leticia Valle:* Questions of Gender and Generation,' *Experimental Writing by Hispanic Women Writers, Monographic Review/Revista Monográfica* 8 (1992): 79–98. In English, Valle-Inclán's *Sonata de invierno* has been published as *Sonata of Winter* in *The Pleasant Memoirs of the Marquis de Bradomín,* trans. May Heywood Broun and Thomas Walsh (New York: Harcourt Brace, 1924).

19. 'Convulsiones de la unidad humana que . . . lucha consigo mismo para conocerse mediante el diálogo' (Rosa Chacel, 'Mujer en galeras,' in *Los títulos,* ed. Clara Janés [Barcelona: Edhasa, 1981], 203).

20. Rosa Chacel, *La confesión* (Barcelona: Edhasa, 1971), 19. Further references to this work are given in parentheses in the text.

21. Chacel, 'Mujer en galeras,' 204.

22. Chacel had explained, for example, (*La confesión,* 23), that *Don Quijote* arose from Cervantes' conclusion that 'in order to believe and to love you must be insane' (*'para creer y amar hay que estar loco'*; original emphasis).

23. 'El movimiento erótico . . . es el mismo hacia toda cosa o ser amado' ('La mujer en el siglo XX,' *Tiempo de Historia* 67 [1980]: 64–81); rpt. in Mori, *Rebañaduras,* 45).

24. Chacel discussed this mutual attraction in an address she delivered on the occasion of receiving an honorary doctorate at the University of Valladolid ('Discurso de la doctora Rosa Chacel,' *Acto de Investidura de Doctora 'Honoris Causa' de Doña Rosa Chacel* [Valladolid: Universidad de Valladolid, 1989], 33).

25. Glenn ('Fiction and Autobiography,' 291) also remarks on Leticia's self-absorption and 'lack of sensitivity.'

26. 'Esquema de los problemas prácticos y actuales del amor,' *Revista de Occidente* 31 (1931): 129–80. Further references to this article are given in parentheses in the text.

27. 'Lograr la perfecta correlación entre las nociones esenciales del amor que poseemos y nuestros procesos y reacciones eróticos' ('Esquema,' 129).

28. Bordons and Kirkpatrick, 'Chacel's *Teresa,*' 289–90.

29. A recent comment by Chacel confirms this indirectly. Speaking of Leticia and 'her loves or, rather, her lovers [sus amores o, más bien, sus amantes],' she recalls creating her protagonist 'as a love-charged pole, where the magnetism of other lives comes and goes [como polo de amor, donde va y viene el magnetismo de otras vidas]' ('Discurso,' 33).

30. Thus Leticia is continually torn between Luisa's abilities and those of Daniel, and she cannot be described as 'faithful' to either of their spheres of influence. She is attracted to people who work with skill, regardless of the task they perform and regardless of their gender. This unspecified attraction, I would suggest, is linked clearly to the homoeroticism Elizabeth Scarlett has stressed in Leticia ('Spanish Women Writers and the Reconquest of Inner Space: Gender,

the Body, and Sexuality in Novels by Emilia Pardo Bazán, Rosa Chacel, and Mercè Rodoreda,' diss., Harvard University, 1991, 113–17) and to Leticia's admiration for the virile femininity she finds in Margarita Velayos. I agree with Scarlett that the homoeroticism in Chacel's work merits further study, in particular Leticia's simultaneous attraction to Daniel and her identification with him: her attraction to Luisa, that is, as if she (Leticia) were a man — something Daniel notes cruelly.

31. Not unrelated to this is Luisa's evident dissatisfaction with her very limited 'world,' despite her efforts to restrain Leticia within it.

32. 'Pretendo lo imposible: hacer que el lector comprenda lo que yo ni siquiera miento' (quoted in Ana Rodríguez, 'Un sistema que el amor presidía,' *Quimera* 84 [December 1984]: 32).

33. 'Deseo de encontrar la mejor femineidad en la inteligente hombría'; 'la mujer perfecta . . . tendría que ser un hombre' (Villena, *'Memorias de Leticia Valle:* La seducción inversa,' 43).

34. Reyes Lázaro, 'Dos concepciones de la memoria: Anámnesis vs. antimemoria uterina en *Desde el amanecer* de Rosa Chacel,' paper read at the Midwest Modern Language Convention, St. Louis, 7 November 1992.

35. 'Si te parece que soy machista, puede que lo sea' (Shirley Mangini, 'Entrevista con Rosa Chacel,' *Insula* 42 [November 1987]: 19).

36. Abigail Lee Six, 'Perceiving the Family: Rosa Chacel's *Desde el amanecer,'* in *Feminist Readings on Spanish and Latin-American Literature*, ed. L. P. Condé and J. M. Hart (Lewiston: Edwin Mellen, 1991), 83, 86–87.

37. Albrecht Neubert, *Text and Translation* (Leipzig: Verlag Enzyklopädie, 1985), 175.

38. Richard Sieburth, 'The Guest: Second Thoughts on Translating Hölderlin,' in *The Art of Translation*, ed. Rosanna Warren (Boston: Northeastern University Press, 1989), 243.

39. Ibid.

40. Mario Parajón, 'Personajes, situaciones y objetos imaginarios en 1945,' *Cuadernos Hispanoamericanos* 270 (December 1972): 527–42.

41. *Lolita* was fist published in 1955, but Nabokov tells of beginning to think about the novel 'late in 1939 or early in 1940' ('On a Book entitled *Lolita,'* *Lolita* [New York: Vintage Books, 1989], 311).

42. 'Traducir la obra de Racine al castellano es empresa de dificultad indiscutible, pero una vez que se la acomete, la tarea proporciona tal placer que desaparece la idea de dificultad' (Rosa Chacel, '*Fedra* en español,' in Rosa Chacel, *La lectura es secreto* [Madrid: Ediciones Júcar, 1989], 191).

Other volumes in the European Women Writers Series include:

Artemisia
By Anna Banti
Translated by Shirley D'Ardia
Caracciolo

*Bitter Healing: German Women
Writers from 1700 to 1830
An Anthology*
Edited by Jeannine Blackwell
and Susanne Zantop

The Maravillas District
By Rosa Chacel
Translated by d. a. démers

The Book of Promethea
By Hélène Cixous
Translated by Betsy Wing

*The Terrible but Unfinished
Story of Norodom Sihanouk,
King of Cambodia*
By Hélène Cixous
Translated by Juliet Flower
MacCannell, Judith Pike, and
Lollie Groth

Maria Zef
By Paola Drigo
Translated by Blossom
Steinberg Kirschenbaum

Woman to Woman
By Marguerite Duras and
Xavière Gauthier
Translated by
Katherine A. Jensen

*Hitchhiking
Twelve German Tales*
By Gabriele Eckart
Translated by Wayne Kvam

The Tongue Snatchers
By Claudine Herrmann
Translated by Nancy Kline

Mother Death
By Jeanne Hyvrard
Translated by Laurie Edson

The House of Childhood
By Marie Luise Kaschnitz
Translated by Anni Whissen

*The Panther Woman
Five Tales from the
Cassette Recorder*
By Sarah Kirsch
Translated by Marion Faber

*Daughters of Eve
Women Writing from the German
Democratic Republic*
Edited by Nancy Lukens and
Dorothy Rosenberg

*On Our Own Behalf
Women's Tales from Catalonia*
Edited by Kathleen McNerney

*Absent Love
A Chronicle*
By Rosa Montero
Translated by Cristina de la
Torre and Diana Glad

The Delta Function
By Rosa Montero
Translated by Kari A. Easton
and Yolanda Molina Gavilan

Music from a Blue Well
By Torborg Nedreaas
Translated by Bibbi Lee

Nothing Grows by Moonlight
By Torborg Nedreaas
Translated by Bibbi Lee

Why Is There Salt in the Sea?
By Brigitte Schwaiger
Translated by Sieglinde Lug

The Same Sea as Every Summer
By Esther Tusquets
Translated by
Margaret E. W. Jones